PLANTS

A NOVEL

Fred Bigjim

Plants

ISBN: 0-7392-0496-3
Library of Congress Catalog Card Number: 99-97157

Printed in the United States by:
Morris Publishing
3212 East Highway 30
Kearney, NE 68847
1-800-650-7888

The Magistrates who redress wrong:
You know that they are not kindly
On that day of righting wrong,
In that hour when they convene.

The Teaching of Merykare
1st Intermediate Period of
Ancient Egypt (c. 2000 B.C.E.)

Dedicated to the
Memory of
Bill Muller

This novel is fully and wholly a work of fiction.
The characters, incidents, events, names, situations,
and dialogue are solely the author's creations.

Other books and works by the author:

Letters To Howard: an interpretation of the Alaska Native Land Claims — co-authored with James Ito Adler

Sinrock

Walk the Wind

We Talk, You Yawn

Echoes from the Tundra

The Last Native (a three act play)

The Long Glass — work in progress

ICONS — work in progress

Prologue

The stars twinkled in the deep midwestern night as the shadowy figure of a man scaled the fence guarding the weapons facility. An alarm shattered the silence and brilliant searchlights sought out the intruder. He ran across the wheat field, and signaled for help, with security agents in pursuit of him. Had the searchlights found him, those watching would have seen him transform from a man into an alien creature; his neck stretching, his torso twisting into a flattened form with a hole through the center, his head disappearing into the shimmering light which seemed to float over the field. He pressed a button on his wrist-watch transmitter, sending his message to one of the blinking stars above. The star blinked back, and swooped past, flattening the wheat into strange hieroglyphs behind it as it soared back into space to turn around. The intruder smiled. In a moment, the blinking star would retrieve him....

Without warning, another of the twinkling lights showed itself to be no star, but an enemy craft, attacking the creature's command ship. The blast from the enemy ship crippled his escape from earth, at least until another ship could be sent to retrieve him.

He could see above him the lightning flashes of the battle between the two craft. A fiery flash illuminated the night and a silvery cylinder escaped from the conflagration and into the darkness of space. The creature's hope of rescue vanished with it. He resumed his human disguise, shifting his plans.

The creature was certain the explosion meant his command ship had been attacked. He could not have known that his lifeline, in escaping from the fireball, had caused the fall of a secret weapon which crashed near the installation he had just fled. Debris from the explosion sent streaks of light shooting across the night sky like stars sinking behind the horizon.

He had little time to ponder the situation or its consequences. Other lights appeared, bobbing slightly in the hands of the installation agents as they ran across the darkened fields in search of him. He quickly made his way toward the nearby hills where he could seek cover.

When morning dawned, a wheat farmer reported finding a new crop circle in his field. The creature's message to the command ship had gone unread. He escaped into the deep recesses of a hidden cave in the deep canyons. Sam Going Away met him there and brought the stranger to his home.

Chapter 1

David Seabird sat in his Los Angeles Sun Times cubicle reading the text of the wire news service story scrolling down his computer screen. It told of a person found wandering at the edge of an Indian reservation in South Dakota.

According to the story, the police were on his trail, suspicious he had broken into a government installation. They followed him onto the Reservation and lost track of him until the next day when they tracked him with dogs to a Reservation house. An Indian from the Reservation, Sam Going Away, had taken in the stranger and cared for him.

When the State police arrived to take the man away, the Indian refused to reveal where he was, saying the police had no legal authority on the Reservation and the man did not want to go with them. It seemed to be another case for the courts to determine police jurisdiction on Indian reservations. An interesting story, David thought, to add to his growing collection of Indian articles. The phone rang, and he turned away from his desk as he lifted the telephone receiver.

"David Seabird," he said.

"David, this is Ward. I've been given some information about a possible scandal breaking in Hollywood. Don't quite know what all is involved."

"What do you have on it?" David asked.

"Seems that some special effects guy working on some of those UFO shows just got caught with his hand in the till, and it turns out he has some kind of connection, or former connection to the government."

"That sounds like a stretch. What am I supposed to be looking for?" David wondered out loud.

"Dunno for sure. Something sounds fishy, though. There's some scuttle-butt about money laundering. Seems like some illegal funds ended up in this special effects unit. I can't make out why anyone in government would care enough about movie and television special effects to risk another Iran-Contra scandal. Especially for something as wonky as outer space fantasies," Ward rambled to himself. "Let me know if there is a story."

"Ok, Ward," David sighed.

Another celebrity chase. Or at least another Hollywood looky-loo. Ward, as Editor-in-Chief, had given David many good assignments in the past six years. This was a great job to land just out of UCLA's journalism school. David thought he had earned Ward's respect, but some of his recent assignments had been of no journalistic importance — ambulance chasing, celebrity chasing, society news.

David actually hoped this might turn out to be something more than some cheap advertising for the latest of Hollywood's space invasions. He gathered his notebooks and walked through the newsroom to the exit.

"Hey, Seabird. Where you off to?"

The voice belonged to the young reporter assigned to cover issues dealing with the homeless and downtrodden. The depressing nature of his assignments never seemed to faze Grant. He had a good sense of humor well matched to his eccentric appearance. His long tangled blond hair resembled the nest of some exotic bird, and his eyes sparkled above the mass of his full beard.

"To the city dump," David replied with a jovial voice.

Grant understood his meaning, for the two shared a distaste for stories based on rumors about the rich and famous. Grant slapped David on the back and laughed gruffly as he replied.

"You should be going to the city dock where all the other seabirds are. I guess there are plenty of seabirds at the dump, too."

Grant laughed at his own joke. David responded by making an obscene gesture toward Grant in an action stripped of meaning by the smile on David's face. The two men were still teasing one another when David turned the corner of the cubicle, his head still turned back toward his colleague. He was startled by a sharp jolt and felt the crunch of a mail cart against his body.

"It serves you right, Seabird," said Grant, who had seen the accident about to happen but had intentionally failed to warn David of the cart's approach.

"Mr. Seabird! I'm so sorry. I didn't see you around the corner. Are you ok?"

A distressed voice which belonged to the mail girl working as an intern squeaked in high-pitched concern. David thought the voice would have been better suited to a different type of girl. He thought it matched a tiny, waif-like girl. Lisa, however, was one of the starting five of her college's girls' basketball team. David looked up at her concerned face and realized how short he felt next to her. He was not tiny, but he seemed small standing beside her.

"It was my fault, Lisa," David assured her.

"It sure was. I'm a witness!" Grant put his arm around Lisa's waist. Grant's head barely reached her shoulders. David could not help but be amused by his short colleague's attempt to comfort the tall girl.

"Some help you are, Grant," David laughed after he spoke. Only his pride was hurt, but Lisa did not look convinced. Her face was crestfallen, almost as if she were fearful she could be fired for reckless driving of a mail cart.

"I should have been watching where I was going," she apologized.

Grant answered for David.

"He got what he deserves for being rude! He should show his friends and buddies more respect!"

David smiled at Lisa and repeated his gesture to Grant. Lisa blushed, and Grant shook his head and laughed as he sent David on his way.

"You better get flying out to the dump before Ward sends you there to live permanently."

David, in a loud whisper meant for Grant's ears, told Lisa, "Next time, make sure you run over him. The rest of the office would take you out to lunch in compensation for your good deed."

David's athletic body, no worse for the accident, glided toward the elevator. He stepped into the blinding light of the city streets, the wind ruffling his sandy brown hair. He turned his squarish face away from the wind, adjusted his round, lightly rimmed glasses which made him look intellectual, but almost hid his striking greenish-gray eyes.

Those eyes caught an advertising display in a window, and David stopped to look more closely at the poster advertising beach houses at Newport. Memories began to flood his mind. His family was from Newport Beach. Although he spent a lot of his years, like others of his age, growing up on the beach, he was different from them, too. He had preferred reading to just hanging out playing volley ball on the beach. He developed many interests and hobbies. He was grateful for his parents' foresight.

His father, as a medical doctor, had volunteered to train public health service personnel in remote villages in Alaska. He had taken David with him on occasion, or had sent him to stay with friends he had made there. David recalled several experiences which had always made him feel special and somehow different from many of his other friends. Not many of them could claim to have had such interesting summer adventures as his. He had camped under the endless Arctic summer sun, rafted down the Kenai River, and taken a canoe trip up part of the Yukon River.

One of the most special memories of these summers in the Alaskan north was of a month-long stay at the village of Sinrock, on the Bering Sea coast. Here, he sat and listened with intense interest to stories of the old Sinrock and King Island Eskimos' trading adventures with Siberian Chuckchi Natives on the other side of the Bering Strait.

The stories culminated in a real adventure of his own. He was given the opportunity to accompany some of the villagers on a walrus hunt. He understood, even then, that he had been given a great honor in being allowed to join the men on this hunt. It was all like a dream.

Although he understood something of the cultural importance of this hunt and the need for food, he also felt sorry for the walrus. David thought he had never seen a creature so magnificent and well-suited to its environment. The Eskimos, too, were part of this environment. David could sense their relationship to the sea, and to the creatures in the sea. He was in awe of the way the men embarked into the vast expanses of ice and water protected only by a thin skin covering stretched over a fragile frame constructed from driftwood. Everything seemed to come from the sea and be a part of the sea.

How different was this way of life on the sea than the one experienced by most of his classmates sunning themselves beside the sea at Newport. His chance to travel and see different cultures had changed him, and his outlook on life. He was curious about other people and places in ways unlike many of his friends. When he could not see something in person, he could read about it. The more David read, the more he began to write. David eventually began to think of writing as a profession.

At the university, he decided to major in journalism, an occupation designed to satisfy many of his varied interests, including Native American issues and cultures. David felt writing could keep him moving in new directions.

David jostled through the crowds of people waiting for the street light to change, thinking how lucky he had been. His family had supported his intellectual interests without questioning his choice of profession. His parents, as professionals, recognized the importance of curiosity and education and had fostered these qualities in him and his sister from the time they were small children. His younger sister was still at Yale, studying for her law degree.

Like David, the rest of his family valued education and all it could bring. His mother was an assistant professor in Art History at the local college, where she specialized in Ancient Egyptian arts. This had introduced David to a completely different world, and had given him an opportunity to see other parts of the world as he accompanied her and the rest of the family on his mother's research trips.

A side benefit of his mother's profession was his relationship with his current girlfriend, Holly. Not many guys could say their mothers had introduced them to their girlfriends, but in a way, his had. Two years before, Holly had been a student in his mother's Egyptian art course, and he had met her with the other students who came to an end-of-term dinner his mother gave for them.

Holly's college degree was in Art History, but she was working as an account executive for one of the leading advertising firms in Los Angeles, specializing in art gallery and museum accounts. She had worked her way up from receptionist through accounts clerk to her current position. It had taken her a number of years, and she worked for the firm all through her years at college.

Holly's dark hair framed her long, narrow face, and her blue eyes could laugh or turn icy cold. When she was excited about a topic, her eyes grew into large pools; when angry they became tiny points of ice almost hidden in the slits her eyelids formed over them. She seemed always to be busy doing or reading something, and her energy was contagious. David smiled as he walked, thinking to himself that it was impossible to win an argument with her, but he sometimes tried anyway.

They shared an interest in the unusual, mysterious, and nonconventional. Both were fascinated by Native American art, culture, and mythology. The books and articles they each read provided material for many lively dinner conversations. Now, they were both reading about sweathouses and how this tradition is practiced in various tribes from the northern plains to the southwest.

He glanced at the sign above a restaurant window, and with a start, remembered he was supposed to meet Holly for lunch. Well,

Ward put an end to that. He pulled the cell phone from his belt and dialed her number. Holly's secretary answered.

"Hi, Meaghan, this is David. Is Holly in?" David asked.

"Hi, David. Sorry, but she is in a conference. You just missed her by a few minutes, and I don't think she will be back in the office until almost noon. Can I take a message for her?" Meaghan apologized in her official and businesslike manner.

"Yeah, tell her I am not going to be able to make it for lunch. She'll just have to get another date for a free lunch!" David's quip did not hide his disappointment, but he knew it was not Meaghan's fault that Holly was out.

Meaghan laughed and said she would see that Holly received the message as soon as possible. David hung up the phone and made a mental note to tell Holly about the article he had read that morning.

He walked into the downtown police division office and greeted the desk sergeant. Because David was there so often, they knew each other on a first name basis and had formed a mutual friendship.

Leon Jefferson had been a street cop, and a very good one. About six years earlier, he had been wounded in the leg and it never healed properly. His limp was noticeable when he moved about the office. Leon was huge, like a street cop ought to be. His teeth gleamed as he smiled broadly and his dark eyes sparkled.

His positive influence in the African-American neighborhoods during his time on the streets made him a small legend. Kids still looked up to him as a role model. He had kept his contacts in these communities after his injury. He had a way of always finding out what was going on there.

"Hey, Seabird. What brings you down here today?" Leon Jefferson's booming drawl echoed across the large, spacious room.

David responded to Leon's welcome, "My editor sent me down to check out the special effects guy you folks brought in for questioning."

Leon laughed and drawled, "Too late, man. The lawyer's got a gag order out. But I'll tell you it ain't no movie star."

"I didn't say I was looking for a movie star, did I?" David quipped, he green eyes searching for hidden meaning behind Leon's own veiled black ones.

"You always are, though, so just thought I'd give you some inside information to keep you happy," Leon growled, his smile contradicting the gruffness in his voice.

"Doesn't help me a bit when you give me information I already have. If it's not a movie star, who is it, and why is he here?" David persisted, hopeful that Leon with give him something.

"Well, David. You're just going to have to become an investigative reporter. Like the rich and famous. we're not supposed to talk to you news vultures."

David reacted with pretended shock. "Vultures? How can you call us vultures?"

"You all tryin' to make a sensation in your paper of those poor stars' little problems?" Leon then became serious as he conveyed to David the notion this was something different; he wasn't going to be able to tell him much.

"Embezzlement and money laundering is not so little a problem is it?" David fished for confirmation of Ward's suspicions. Leon's eyes betrayed not even a hint of what he actually thought.

"Not my problem to make other people's problems my business," Leon drawled. "I'm just the desk clerk here. Talk to the judge."

David feigned a hurt expression, and replied.

"Ah, come on. Can't you just give me a hint? I have to take something back to the editor. You must know something about the charges. They have to charge them with something when they bring them in here, and you must see that charge."

Leon wouldn't budge.

David leaned over the desk as he pretended to give Leon a bit of confidential information.

"This could be the scoop of the century. You could get your 15 minutes of fame here," David said.

Leon held up his hands as if backing away from David's pretended corrupting influence. There wasn't the usual lightness, though, in the action. Something was different. Leon seemed slightly uneasy about the whole thing, and David almost felt like there was a warning in Leon's voice when he answered.

"Don't need fame, need retirement. Besides, they excused me for this one. I wasn't in on it. Seems a bit strange, come to think of it. But I get paid the same whether I'm here or not." Leon replied. "You might want to think about not being in on it, too. Just go back to your editor and tell him there's no story. Some things just aren't worth pursuing, you know."

David stared into Leon's black eyes, searching for the meaning behind Leon's statement. Leon looked away and towards the window. A momentary pause settled on the room as David, puzzled by the encounter with his friend, sat in the chair in front of Leon's desk. Leon rose and walked to the coffee machine. He returned with a couple of cups and offered one to David and changed the subject.

"Hey, David, isn't a vulture a bird?" Leon asked, trying to lighten the pall that had settled over the atmosphere.

"Yeah, why?" David looked up, still puzzled, as he sipped the coffee. The extreme change of subject caught him off guard.

"Just wondering if Seabirds and vultures are related," Leon said as he smiled at David.

David continued to look over the rim of his cup at Leon, not sure what to make of his statement. Leon continued.

"What is the difference between a Hermann's Seagull and a garbage dump seagull?"

"Is there a difference?" David said. "I thought seagulls were all the same."

"A garbage dump seagull eats garbage," Leon said in a serious voice, followed by a peal of raucous laughter.

Leon's voice boomed as he enjoyed his little joke. The laughter subsided, and he continued, still in a non-serious vein.

"I hope garbage is not what you're poking around here for today."

"For garbage? Right, Leon. You should be a comedian instead of a desk sergeant. Then I could write the review of your act." David smiled at Leon and took another sip of coffee. He again sensed that behind the joke, Leon was somehow warning him away from any further investigation of this particular story.

David finished his coffee and rose to leave.

"If you're not going to help me, I guess I'll just have to go back to work empty-handed and tell the boss I couldn't get past Leon's desk."

Leon's laughter boomed again, but there was no sparkle in his eyes.

"Sorry I can't help, buddy, but it's my job, Seabird. Try to stay out of the garbage!"

David smiled and waved good-bye and Leon greeted a person who passed David in the doorway. David walked down the street and stopped by the local diner for a sandwich. He puzzled over Leon's strange attitude as he munched his lunch. As he thought about the conversation, he couldn't escape the thought that Leon knew something about this case and had warned him away from any kind of involvement in it.

By the time David returned to the office, Ward was gone for lunch. David sighed his relief that he did not have to tell Ward that there was no story.

A note on his desk informed him that Holly had called while he was out. He pulled out the article on Sam Going Away and phoned her. The sparkle in her voice lifted the feelings of anxiety and depression which had settled over him after his unproductive conversation with Leon. "Can we get together later?" David asked Holly at the end of their exchange of news.

"It is the reason I wanted you to call," Holly replied. "One of my clients is having an opening at his gallery tonight. Want to come along?"

"More society types getting together?" David was being facetious, but he did not enjoy these functions much. They seemed to him to be places where people went to impress others rather than to appreciate the art.

Holly tried to give him a bit of encouragement. "No, not so high scale," she said. "He represents good artists — some are modern. I know you don't like much of the modern art, but he has North American Indian art, too. I know you'll find those interesting, and a few of the Native American artists will be there."

"Yeah, I'd like to meet them." David's voice began to betray a genuine interest.

"I thought you would. Who knows, it might give you some other connections you could use someday. I know you're always looking for those." Holly was serious about the first statement, but said the second with ironic humor.

"You don't need to be so sarcastic." David was not offended, but his voice took on a similar vein of irony.

"Just the truth, dearie," she responded.

"I need to bring you back to reality," David said with a more serious voice. "There was an article on the wire service today about an Indian in South Dakota I'd like to interview someday. This old man, Sam Going Away, seems to be involved in some dispute about the rights of Indians on their own lands and protection against outside police interference. We've got to follow this one and see how it turns out. It sounds like any decision on it might affect other areas, too."

"A decision on it could be important," Holly agreed.

She paused for a moment in reflection, and added, "He has such an intriguing name. I wonder how he or his ancestors came to have such a name. I'm sure it must have significance."

David answered, “Yeah, I think so. I’m glad to know other people have unusual names, and not just me.”

Holly resumed a light-hearted manner, “Shall I meet you there or do you want to pick me up about 6:30 in your limousine?”

“I’ll pick you up, but you’ll have to settle for a Fairmont instead of a limo.” David said before he hung up.

David went back to work feeling frustrated that he was not able to get any information for Ward about the movie star, or whatever the person was. He phoned a couple of sources to see if they knew anything, but either they knew nothing, or were too scared of a lawsuit to say anything.

David went out for a coffee and returned with it to his desk. He sipped it slowly as he relaxed. He sat back with his feet on the desk and gazed out the window.

The shrill ring of his telephone startled him and he jumped, spilling hot coffee on his arm.

“Dammit,” he muttered as he tried to wipe coffee off his sleeve and the papers on his desk, while at the same time grabbing the phone.

“Yeah, Seabird,” he half shouted into the phone.

“I hear you’ve been down at the police station asking questions,” a deep voice said.

“Yeah, I was down there today. Who’s this?” David asked.

“Doesn’t matter. What *does* is that you aren’t minding your own business,” the man continued.

“It’s my job,” David said. He was getting annoyed. “Who is this?” he asked again.

“You listen to me. You quit poking around in things that don’t concern you, or you’ll find yourself in more trouble than you can imagine,” the man threatened.

“What’s that supposed to mean,” David asked.

“Just how it sounds. Leave it alone,” the man continued.

“Leave what alone?” David was becoming concerned.

"You know what. Drop your investigation on this assignment or your friends and family will be attending a very sad event," the man said ominously.

"There isn't any investigation," David said flatly.

"Keep it that way," the man replied and hung up.

David held the receiver in his hand, almost expecting the voice to return. When he regained his composure, he dialed his secretary.

"Jenny, could you find out the number of the caller you just put through to me?" he asked.

"Sure, Mr. Seabird," she replied. Within moments, she came back with the number. It had a Seattle prefix.

Why, David wondered, would someone in Seattle care about the arrest of someone in LA? Or care enough to threaten his life. It almost made him want even more to know who the person was and why they had been arrested. He had the feeling it wasn't just the charges these people cared about. And he knew about taking threats seriously. Sometimes people had a lot to lose by having secrets disclosed, and that made them dangerous. He also knew little mistakes could lead to big problems — the Watergate break-in, for instance. Who would have anticipated where it led? It left him chilled.

Chapter 2

David, still unnerved by the telephone call, realized he had to pick up Holly as planned. Her office was in an upscale glass high-rise with security guards at the front door to direct traffic. Wally, the security guard on duty, recognized David with a greeting and called Holly to let her know David was waiting.

Wally was heavyset and balding. He leaned back against his chair with an air of relaxed self-importance.

"How's your work going, son?" Wally said with genuine interest. "Are you working on something good?"

Wally's voice was low and coarse. David thought it sounded like a man who had spent many years smoking cigars. David's impression of Wally was of a somewhat paternalistic man, in the positive sense. Wally took a fatherly concern in the business of everyone who came through the building or who worked there.

"Going good," David lied.

The elevator door opened and Holly appeared. She greeted David with a kiss. "Hi, honey. Ready for a little culture?" She winked at Wally, who smiled appreciatively at her attention to him.

"Good night, kids. You have a good evening now." Wally waved as he spoke.

"Where are we headed?" David asked as they stepped into his car.

"It's out by UCLA," Holly answered. "It's called 'Canterbury's' and the guy who owns it has an account with our agency. He has eclectic tastes — gets a little of everything in there." Holly paused, then continued, her fluttering hands saying almost as much as her voice. "I think some of the artists he is showing now are supposed to be up-and-coming. He shows a lot of aspiring artists, and many of them become important. He seems to have a talent for choosing good artists."

David was already on the road. Holly continued enthusiastically, her lively manner apparent in the sparkle of her large eyes and in the movement of her long, thin fingers.

"One of the things I like about him is the way he embraces aboriginal and Native American arts. He treats the artists as artists, instead of just saying their arts are 'crafts,' or 'ethnography.' He puts them on the same level as Monet or Warhol — you know, artists."

David interjected, "What is tonight's function?"

Holly answered, "It's an opening to honor several young contemporary Australian Aboriginal and North American Indian artists. Should be interesting."

"Don't you think this guy is exploiting them by putting their art in the commercial market." David resented dealers who took advantage of their artists.

"I don't think so," Holly replied. She praised her client ethics as well as his tastes.

"He seems to respect both the art and the artists. Besides, they should have a chance to show their art and get paid something fair for it the same as other artists do."

"Yeah, I know," David agreed. "It seems like Native artists are too often cheated by those who claim to represent them."

"By the public, too," Holly said. "Their work gets stuck in ethnography departments of museums or put in tourist shops instead of fine arts galleries. Even if they become famous as fine artists, they don't often get the high prices other artists can command."

David was glad to be in Holly's company. Her conversation took his mind off the troubling call and helped him relax a bit. After fighting the traffic and trying to find some place to park the car, they joined the rest of the gallery patrons streaming into the three-story building which housed the gallery.

The gallery had several rooms, and in the center of the main one was a long table filled with platters of sandwiches, hors d'oeuvres, champagne, wine, coffee and tea. The patrons were served by uniformed staff, after which they took their glasses and plates and circulated around the gallery exchanging small talk with the other art-lovers.

David and Holly, wine glasses in hand, strolled from one work of art to another. The gallery was filled with the low murmur of voices as patrons discussed the art and gossiped among themselves. They were soon greeted by the owner of the gallery, who was busy mingling with each of his guests.

"Good evening, Holly. I'm so pleased you could make it to the opening tonight. Isn't it a fabulous show? I'm just so excited. You must meet my artists."

David cringed at the high-pitched voice and affected manner of his host. The greeting was punctuated by strong accents which made the voice almost musical, David thought. The emphasis on the words, "so" and "must," made them dominate the phrases, and they continued to ring in David's ears as Holly's voice interrupted his thoughts.

"Tony, I'd like you to meet David Seabird. He's the journalist I told you about."

Holly reached for David's arm and pulled him forward. David extended his hand to clasp Tony's in a handshake.

"David, Tony Kerr." Holly completed the introduction.

"Pleased to meet you, David. What was your last name again?" Tony cocked his head to one side as if trying to hear above the noise of the crowd around them.

"Seabird," David repeated.

"Is your name Native American?" asked Tony.

"Yes, it's Native American in one sense. I'm a Native of America, but I'm not a Native American." David replied with subtle irony.

Tony looked puzzled for a moment, then broke into a broad smile.

"You must come and meet some of our Native American artists. I believe they will relate to you with such a name."

Tony took Holly's arm, and, immediately sidetracked, led them to some of his favorite works in the show. Tony chattered endlessly about each work they passed, extolling the virtues of first this painting, then those prints, and now this sculpture. He certainly loved his job.

David could see how he could be a good salesman, but he was glad he did not have to work with him all the time.

Tony discussed some of the details of the exhibition. Tony and Holly had talked earlier about the possibility of a review for the show's opening. Holly thought David might be able to help, especially with his interests in Native American arts and myths.

David reassured Tony he would do what he could.

"I'll tell my co-worker, Jan Ingraham, to make sure she does a good piece on this show. She often does gallery reviews and I think she would be interested in this."

Hors d'oeuvres in hand, Tony guided Holly and David to the opposite side of the gallery where a young Native American stood.

"Seegook," said Tony, "I'd like to introduce David Seabird and Holly Kingston. This is Seegook, one of our featured artists tonight."

Seegook smiled and extended his hand first to David and then to Holly. Tony continued with the introductions.

"David is a journalist at the L.A. Sun-Times, and has agreed to give us some good press." He glanced with a smile at David, who returned a non-committal grin.

Tony continued his explanation, "Holly keeps our advertising account in order. We depend on her." Holly took Seegook's hand in greeting while thanking Tony for his compliment to her. Tony made his apologies after completing the introductions and returned to circulate among his other guests.

Seegook was in his mid-20's, at least as far as David could judge. His long black hair was pulled back into a pony-tail, and the dark eyes in his round, olive-colored face reflected his

Eskimo heritage. The hooded anorak hung about his medium frame.

"I'm from the Bering Sea coast of Alaska," Seegook responded to David's questions about his background. "I know what they teach in Art Institutes, but my main source of inspiration was my uncle and his teachings."

Seegook explained that his uncle had been an important ivory carver and one of the last shamans in that region. He said in his soft, accented voice, "My uncle's influence can be seen in most of my paintings, prints, and sculptures on display in this gallery."

David, taking Holly by the hand, followed Seegook to one of the paintings hanging on the wall.

David scrutinized the work. The image was of a walrus-man. It looked sculpted, with two thin stick-like legs that disappeared beneath a brown skin coat. Two flippers with extensions like fingers were held up like those of a blessing priest. David was not sure if the extensions were fingers or hands.

The head was of a human being, but from the upper lips grew walrus tusks. The human-like image had an eerie, alien quality to it as it floated in a groundless sky.

Seegook noticed David's intense interest in the painting and said, "Here is what I mean when I said my uncle's ivory carvings inspired me. I used to sit beside him and watch him carve seals, walruses, and other sea creatures. They always had a human personality."

Seegook paused, reflecting on his memories before he continued. "My uncle would tell me the myths of my Inupiaq people. There was the sea-goddess who transforms herself into a seal. There are sky gods and shamans that fly through the sky."

Seegook brought David and Holly to a framed print and said, "This is an example."

The print showed a flying figure with outstretched arms. The arms had birds and land animals on them as if they were hitching a ride. In the center of this airborne human-seal figure was a reindeer spirit with antlers looking out through what seemed to be a hole in the human figure's stomach.

David and Holly stood in silence looking at the print in awe.

Seegook continued, "My uncle told me a story about earth men going to the moon. The journey was nothing new to him."

David glanced at Holly in surprise. David asked Seegook, "Are you talking about when NASA put men on the moon?"

Holly squeezed David's arm as Seegook replied.

"No, not like our space travel. He was talkin' about the shamans who could fly and go anywhere, even to the moon. They had spirit helpers like reindeer or seals or birds. They had 'Spirit Moves'."

David looked puzzled and asked, "What are 'Spirit Moves'?"

Seegook answered, "'Spirit Moves' is when shamans change themselves into the animals which are their spirit helpers."

Seegook continued, "My uncle carved these figures. Now I put them in paintings, prints, and sculptures."

Holly responded to Seegook's explanation with animation. "It's interesting how so many people around the world have similar traditions. When I was at school, I studied mythology and art, and I was fascinated by the fact that completely different cultures have similar ideas and arts. These X-ray shaman paintings you have done and the X-ray paintings of Australian Aboriginals are so much alike in many ways."

Seegook agreed with Holly as David wandered to a brightly colored painting. It showed a tall, thin figure which stood out against the black background. The neck was long and red. Its arms were stretched over the figure's narrow, oval head. Within the grasp of its hands was a circular form with a face on it. Long rays extended from the circle like rays of the sun. The figure's feet stood on another circle with a face. This was a silvery color, and looked like an image of the moon. The long, white, serpentine legs standing on the moon were covered with feathers. The arms were like feathered wings.

Seegook stood next to David and after a brief pause, spoke about the painting. "This is a spirit in flight. It glides between the sun and the moon. The feathers are of the birds. They are able to fly above the earth."

Seegook led David and Holly to a plain, wooden sculpture called a Flatboard. He spoke as they looked at it. "This sculpture is what inspired the painting we just saw."

The sculpture was made of a large oval ring with two paddles attached to the outside. These were like legs for a figure of a human inside the ring. The oval ring framed a flat board cut into the shape of a human being. Geometric patterns had been cut away from parts of the figure. Seegook continued. "These cutout patterns show the phases of the moon."

David responded, "The pattern of those cutouts makes the board look like a man holding his arms above his head. I can see how much it is like your painting in this way."

"I can't help but remember how many times I've seen this same image in art classes," added Holly. "It seems like it is found all over. I've seen the same symbols in all kinds of art, from Sioux petroglyphs to Russian embroideries. They are even like some of the figures in Navajo sand paintings, aren't they?"

Seegook answered as he gestured toward the sculpture. "One of my classmates at the art institute was Navajo. We used to compare our own peoples' myths and symbols. We found a lot in common."

David's eye caught a tall sculpture nearby. He made his way toward it as Holly and Seegook followed. David walked around it. When he returned to Seegook's side, Seegook began to explain why he had created this work. "I was lookin' at some labrets in a museum one day. They all had stick bodies and these round or oval heads. They looked like flying shamans to me. There was something different about them, too. They were like trees with their arms held up like that."

Holly added, "Like the 'tree of life,' isn't it?"

The main part of the sculpture was a long narrow pole. The top had the familiar round head and long, narrow body with the uplifted arms.

"You are sure you didn't get the inspiration for this from 'ET'?" David asked with a grin.

Seegook smiled a serious smile. "No, I got it from the labrets. I suppose some of it could have come from ET's, though, because there is some of my uncle's talk in it, too. You'd be amazed at some of the stories my uncle told me. You probably wouldn't believe them, though."

Seegook led them on around the gallery, stopping at a simple, abstract painting. He spoke again in his soft voice. "Here's a work you should see, David. It's called 'Seagod'."

The human-like figure was nothing more than a line drawing. Two legs extended from the thin body, and the arms grew from a neck that seemed to be as long as the body. At the top was a "head," with two concentric circles with lines coming out of the outer one.

The radiant lines from the outer circle almost glowed like heat waves or sunlight. It seemed to draw David into the eye of its faceless head.

Seegook began to describe the work. "In this work..." Seegook stopped as he saw David's eyes roll into the back of his head. He caught David's arm, preventing his collapse but not in time to catch the glass which fell from his hand to crash on the floor.

David was unaware of these events. He heard the sound of trumpeting swans, then felt himself soaring above the crowd. He could see through the bodies of those beneath him; he felt set apart from them, but one with swans which seemed to fly with him. He soared through the roof and beyond the clouds. As suddenly as it had begun, he was back in his earth-bound body with Seegook shaking him.

Holly was at his side, clearly concerned about David's health and why he would have fainted.

Seegook's explanation did not put Holly entirely at ease. "He is fine. This is not about David's health, but his future. He had a vision just now. He has been chosen by a shamanic spirit. He will have much to learn, and it will sometimes be dangerous."

"I don't understand," Holly said.

"I'm ok," David reassured her. "It's amazing — fantastic. I'm fine," he mumbled.

"But Seegook says it might be dangerous," Holly said with concern. "Are you sure it was not the wine?" she asked Seegook.

"No, there is something I will have to tell you about. A phone call. I don't know how this fits, but I think it is connected somehow," David said as he recovered his composure.

Holly convinced David they should get some fresh air and then something to eat. She still thought his collapse might be due to a need for food.

" Seegook, I think we'd better go," Holly said.

"Ok, I understand. David has had quite an experience. Not everyone is chosen for such a mission. I will be in touch with you — here or in the spirit world," Seegook promised.

David did not remember how he arrived at the restaurant, but Holly had apparently insisted on his getting something to eat. She was sure he needed food. They waited for their food to be served, Holly quietly watching with concern, and David absently staring at the flames behind the grill.

"Where were you tonight?" Holly asked, looking into the fire reflected in David's eyes. "You seem like you are in another world," she asked. The light flickered in David's eyes as he turned to her and said softly, "I'm thinking about Seegook's painting."

"Seagod?" Holly guessed. "What happened?"

Holly waited for David to explain, but he said nothing more. She reached for a carrot from the bowl of vegetables before them. "What was it about the painting? What happened to you?"

She searched for a way to draw David's explanation from him. "I'm not sure," David replied. "It's something about the painting and what it means. It's about the message it keeps giving me. All of Seegook's works had a kind of theme running through them. I can't quite place what it is, but there's something there which touches me. It moved me."

"I know it moved you. You fainted." Holly looked into David's eyes with wonder. She was seeing a different side of David and was filled with genuine interest about David's thoughts and feelings.

"I didn't feel like I fainted. I felt conscious of everything. It was as if I was flying with swans. In fact, it almost seemed I went to Alaska and was soaring over the tundra, over Sinrock. When I was a kid, I spent a few weeks there, way up north on the Bering Sea coast. It was quite an adventure for me," David began to explain. "While I was there, an old Eskimo ivory carver took a grandfatherly interest in me. He was well known as a carver and was said to be shaman. The rest of the villagers seemed to have great respect for him," David continued.

He paused, buttered a piece of bread, took a few bites in silence, and continued his story. "I used to sit with him in his house and watch him work. He would tell me stories as he carved, just like I was a grandson. He would explain through the stories why he was carving something, and what it was supposed to mean. I had forgotten about Old Man Koongoosuk until I saw Seegook's painting. When I saw 'Seagod,' I remembered the old man and his ivory carvings. It was almost like a carving he made years ago when I was there with him. I almost thought I saw him again, looking at me from somewhere, in some other dimension or something."

Holly watched David's face with fascination. She could almost see the memories flooding his mind. David continued.

"The story the old man told me then," David paused in thought, "it was the same."

"The same as what?" Holly pressed for David's answer.

"The same as Seegook's," David said. "I was thinking about the story of the shaman flying to the moon. I had forgotten it.

Koongoosuk told me he had flown to the moon. When I was a kid, I just thought it was a story. I didn't know anything about mythology or religion. I only thought it was another fairy tale. Maybe he was telling me the truth."

Holly, in stunned surprise, sat with fork in hand for a moment, set it down, and reached across the table for David's hand. "David, what a lovely thought. It is such a rich memory to find again. I was really worried about you, you know. I thought you were having a stroke or something." She squeezed David's hand. He smiled at her and said, "I thought you might think it was silly of me to tell you this. You know, maybe I was starting to believe fairy tales or something." He felt a warm glow, supported by her confidence in him.

"I'm glad you remembered the old man," she said.

"Something else happened when I was looking at the painting." Holly waited for David to continue.

David's voice trembled as he spoke. Holly stroked his hand and gazed into his moist eyes. "I can see why you said it moved you. One doesn't get a visit from the past every day," she said, herself overcome with emotion by David's story.

David said quietly, "Old man Koongoosuk called me by name when I saw him. He called me by the name he gave me, Seagoyuk. I know it was him. No one else knows me by that name."

David paused, looking down at his plate, then spoke softly, "He gave me a warning. He told me there is danger ahead. Danger from the skies."

Chapter 3

Saturday was another hot, sunny day of early summer. David was awakened by his cat, Bastet, jumping up beside him on the bed. Bastet settled herself near his head and began to purr. She seemed to be protective, somehow, as if aware of the unease he had felt since the events of the previous evening.

The sun was streaming into the bedroom from the east window, giving the room a false coziness. David heard the song of a bird drifting into his room from down the hall, reminding him he had forgotten to cover the bird's cage when he came home. Maybe that was why it had seemed distressed during the night.

David stroked the cat's fur, thinking about the events of the previous evening. He realized that Bastet's purring and the simple action of petting her made him relax. Bastet looked up at him and he felt he could almost read her thoughts and her his.

David marveled at the strange and wonderful relationship of pets and their owners. He smiled at the fond memory of his eccentric great-aunt, Miriam, and her dog, Muffin. David remembered his aunt treated the dog like the child she never had. Long before pet shops were selling raincoats and booties for animals, Aunt Miriam was creating special outfits for Muffin.

David recalled how Aunt Miriam swore by Muffin's special gift to foretell events, from changes in weather to the arrival of unexpected guests. Once, she claimed, she was tending the baby chicks in a brooder house when the door was blown open by a breeze. The chicks scattered and she raced after them, scooping up as many as she could.

Muffin watched her a few moments, and began to herd the little birds into groups and stood guard, barking for attention, until Aunt Miriam retrieved them. When all but one had been collected, Aunt Miriam started to look for the last chick. Muffin cocked her head, seemed to grasp the problem still facing Aunt Miriam, and put her nose to the ground in a search for the chick.

The dog found it hiding under a large leaf. She put her paw gently on the leaf, holding the chick in place, and barked until Aunt Miriam came to collect it.

Aunt Miriam had been surprised at Muffin's behavior, but not at her intelligence. Muffin had done other amazing things, but Aunt Miriam thought the incident had shown the depth of many animals' uncanny abilities to understand human thought.

David had often thought of Aunt Miriam's eccentricities, or at least what many in his family thought were eccentricities. He, however, thought she was right in many ways. Her trust in her pets was founded on years of experience. She treated them well, and they, in turn, gave her a remarkable understanding of their ability to communicate with human beings.

Aunt Miriam had once told him animals should not be seen as mere pets. They, she said, were beings put on this earth to assist humans in many ways. It was this reason, she believed, doctors would someday find pets valuable for treating patients with conditions ranging from high blood pressure to low self-esteem.

He had remembered Aunt Miriam when a stray cat arrived in the neighborhood. David was the only one who showed kindness to the cat, and as a result the cat chose to adopt him. Holly had chosen the name. Once the cat entered the house, she said, she ruled it, just like a goddess. She should be called Bastet, Holly had said, after the ancient Egyptian cat goddess.

The bird, too, had been a stray of sorts. David never knew how it arrived where it was when he found it, shivering and cold on a rain-soaked street. He was working late one winter day, and as he left, he saw the bird waddling from shop to shop trying to find a safe, dry doorway in which to hide from the storm.

He ran back to the office for a box, and slowly approached the bird. It seemed almost happy to see him, and he brought it back to his house for the weekend. He advertised his find, but no one responded to his notice about a lost bird. Therefore, he and the bird adopted each other.

Holly named him, too. The bird was like the figure in Greek myth who flew too close to the sun and was destroyed. She said the bird should be called, "Icarus," and so it was.

David had been concerned about bringing the bird home, as the natural instinct of a cat is to hunt birds. Bastet, however, seemed to accept the bird as part of David's life and never made any attempt to harm the bird. David could almost hear Aunt Miriam say, of course the cat would accept the bird, because it was rescued by David just as the cat had been.

David thought his animals' behavior was uncharacteristic the last few hours. Bastet had paced the room all night, and seemed disturbed by something he could not see. Icarus fluttered and squawked as if afraid. David remembered the old shaman in the village telling how animals could predict events, like storms and earthquakes, but could also foretell what was to happen in a person's life, especially someone close to them who is in danger. It as if Icarus and Bastet sensed something about his experience the night before.

The phone rang, interrupting David's thoughts about his pets. Ward's voice sounded strained.

"David, I need to have you come into the office this afternoon. I know it's Saturday, but I've learned of a story which could interest you. I think you'll agree it will be worth your time."

David could not get a word into the conversation until Ward stopped speaking.

"What is it?" David asked when at last Ward gave him an opening.

"I can't tell you right now. Can you make it in this afternoon?" Ward asked.

"Sure. I'll be there at two," David answered.

"Thanks," replied Ward just before he cut the connection.

David hung up the telephone, feeling a vague unease about the assignment. It was more than just the fact of giving up his

Saturday. As he spoke to Ward, Bastet arched her back and began to hiss in distress.

Chapter 4

Ward's door was open, and he glanced up from his work as David entered his office. Ward was tall, thin and bearded. His square glasses rested on his long, thin nose. His graying hair was long and combed back from his face. Like most middle-aged men burdened with great responsibility, Ward always looked a little worried.

He was friendly, though, and supportive of his staff. David knew Ward thought well of him even if he didn't always agree with his suggestions. This was why he was sure Ward was looking for more than the obvious on assignments which at first seemed trivial.

"What's so important to drag me out on a nice sunny Saturday? Are we going fishing?" David asked with a smile.

"You are, as a matter of fact," responded Ward as he poured a cup of coffee and handed it to David. Ward's voice was deep and authoritative. David thought he sounded like the perfect, precise professional announcer for classical music radio stations. Because he dealt with words on paper, he chose those he used in speaking with care.

"What do you mean, I am? You're not coming with me?" David accepted the coffee as he asked Ward the question with a flippant manner.

"This isn't for fish this time, I'm afraid," Ward was unusually reserved. In fact, he sounded almost worried, cautious.

David was intrigued. "What are you talking about?"

"I've got a job for you," said Ward slowly, sipping his coffee during the intervening silence.

He continued, "You are my best investigative reporter, so I thought you would be ideal for this assignment." His eyes met David's over the rim of the coffee cup.

David waited for Ward to go on. He could tell that something about this assignment was bothering Ward. It was almost as if

Ward was having a hard time bringing himself to talk about what it was he was asking David to do.

"Last night, I had a telephone call from one of my old sources in the Pentagon," Ward said. "We served in the military together years ago. I trust him. He was one of my first contacts when I was a green journalist in D. C. and we've kept up our contacts. He's well-placed in the Washington bureaucracy."

"So what does this have to do with my assignment?" David asked.

"Don't be impatient, David. I think you should hear the whole story as I know it. We'll get there," Ward said. He stood up and walked over to the window with his hands behind his back. He gazed out the window in silence. "Just don't ask questions until I finish with this."

David stared nervously at the center of Ward's desk, waiting for Ward to continue. His instincts as a reporter made it difficult for him to sit silently without asking for more information. He lived for information, and for getting it quickly.

"He wouldn't lie to me. He wouldn't have any need to. I know that," Ward said as if trying to convince himself.

Ward walked over to the coffee pot and poured himself another cup. David sipped from his cup and stared into the bottom. The tension David felt in the room had never been between them before. Something seemed wrong — Ward seemed like a stranger to him.

"Now, David, after you hear what I am going to tell you, you know you don't have to take this assignment," Ward said as he sat back down at his desk. He took off his glasses and stared into David's eyes.

"My colleague's problem is one of secrets," Ward said slowly. "It's hard to tell you about this, because we just don't know much. He and a couple of his contacts have uncovered something strange. It looks like a shadow government has set up its own weapons testing program. You can see this has very serious implications."

Ward got up again and paced back over to the window. David waited in silence.

"What did you find out yesterday when you were down at the police station?" Ward's sudden change of topic caught David off guard.

"What does that have to do with weapons testing?" David answered in surprise.

"Maybe nothing, but maybe everything. Did you come up with anything?" Ward asked again.

"Nothing but a stone wall. I don't think Leon knew anything about it either. He just joked around like he usually does when everything is fine. What's going on?" David asked.

"I don't really know, but I think there might be a connection between that incident and what I found out last night." Ward said.

"Tell me more." David said as he gulped his coffee, his interest rising.

"They think there is some big corporate money and very advanced technology coming in from the Northwest region of the U.S., maybe from Seattle." Ward started to relate.

"Really?" David interjected. "I had an interesting call yesterday myself."

Ward stood frozen for a moment, then David continued.

"When I got back, there was a call for me warning me against investigating anything related to the person who had been taken to the station. They sounded pretty serious."

"How serious?" Ward asked.

"Like it could be dangerous to my health to continue." David replied.

"Ok, I think we must be onto something then. We must have rattled a few cages." Ward said.

"But how? We didn't even know we were looking for anything." David thought out loud. "And how does this fit with your information?"

"Yeah, guess I better fill you in on what we know. From what our folks down at the Pentagon have gathered so far, there is speculation that money has been diverted into illegal and secret weapons research. They think there might be a shadow government being set up around it."

"How does this have anything to do with some special effects technician getting arrested for something we know nothing about?" David asked.

"Dunno," Ward replied. "But there must be a connection somewhere. Maybe he used to work for them, or maybe he knows technology or space or weapons systems or something. I guess that is part of what you need to find out."

"Well, what kind of testing are they doing, or do we know?" David poured himself another cup of coffee.

"It has something to do with Tesla-type research — you know, using radio waves, messing around with the atmosphere and weather, the ozone layer — things like that. The potential damage to the environment is almost as critical as the ability of whoever these people are to wage war against our own government or anyone else they choose to aim for."

Ward came back to his desk and sat down again. "I had trouble believing any of this could happen under our noses like this, but these people are convinced they've found something big. If they are right, it IS big. This could be more explosive than Watergate and Iran-Contragate put together."

David looked up at Ward, who stared intently back at him.

"Here's where you come in. My Pentagon source thinks they have isolated the general region where at least one of the secret testing grounds is located. It's near an Indian reservation in South Dakota. Hey, here's where there might be a connection to our special effects guy."

David could see that something important had just dawned on Ward. He waited for Ward to share it with him.

"This facility, it's masking as a Hollywood studio where they produce movies and television programs on UFO's. Supposedly, they have made it into a little research-center, documentary productions facility. So I guess they try to create effects to include in these "documentary" shows and try to convince the gullible public that we have all been visited by aliens. Our folks have infiltrated it. I guess at this center, they are actually creating and testing hi-tech weapons and getting some of the money from this outfit in the Pacific Northwest and through the shadow government somehow."

"Wow," David gulped.

"They think there might be other facilities in New Mexico or Arizona. The inside contacts from South Dakota are working to get more on this, which they hope to have by the time you get there. Of course, that is if you are game."

"When do you want me to leave?" David asked without hesitation.

"Before you say yes, I want to be sure you understand the dangers involved here, David," Ward said slowly.

David felt a rush of adrenaline through his system. How could he not say yes. This was why he had become a reporter in the first place.

"I'll take the assignment, Ward. I understand. You aren't responsible for anything that happens," David said.

"I am ultimately responsible, David," Ward's hands were shaking as he picked up his coffee cup.

David noticed the coffee rippling in Ward's cup and realized he had never seen Ward so nervous in all his years working with him.

"You know, all of this is between you and me, David," Ward said.

"You sound like this is 'Mission Impossible,' and the tape is about to self-destruct in ten seconds, Ward," David said lightly, trying to ease the tension.

Ward's smile was weak and unconvincing. He continued, "I've got to tell my editorial board why I'm spending good money to send you all over the country and what might be a wild goose chase, if we're lucky. I'm going to say you are doing a feature on the Sioux problem in South Dakota."

"Which problem?" David asked, knowing it could be any number of difficulties facing Indian reservations.

"I'm going to say you are looking into the land claims problems and the whole situation with the Black Hills — why they rejected the money, why they want it now. You know, make something out of it, ok?"

"Yeah, I can take care of it," David said confidently. "I've kept up my interest in Indian affairs since I was in Alaska. I can create something if I don't find it."

David paused, then added, "You know, it's an eerie coincidence, but I just read something on the wire service today about an incident on a reservation in South Dakota. It involved an old Indian by the name of Sam Going Away."

Ward looked up and said. "By all means, be careful. Neither of us know just what we're dealing with here."

"When do I leave?" David asked.

"My source can send someone to meet you and give you the credentials to get you into the facility. We could send you to Rapid City tomorrow. Is that a problem?" Ward asked.

"I'll be there," David said, aware of the sound of his pounding heart.

Chapter 5

David packed his bag, loaded the animals into his car, and drove to Holly's apartment. He couldn't tell her much about his assignment. Nor did he want her to be concerned about his safety. It was probably good he could not tell her much.

She met him at the door with a kiss. "You didn't say much about why you were going to South Dakota tomorrow. What's up?"

"Ward's sending me out to investigate a story on an Indian Reservation up there," he answered half-truthfully. He thought of Sam Going Away.

"I'm going to try to meet an old man named Sam Going Away, for one thing," David added.

"What's special about him?" Holly asked.

"It has to do with Indian rights and who has final authority on the reservation. I guess he took in someone who was accused of a crime. The government says he should give him up to be tried in federal court. The Indians say he was on their territory, so they should be have judicial authority. I'm supposed to be checking into land claims problems, too," David said.

During dinner the conversation turned to the exhibition at the gallery they had attended the previous night. David told Holly of a strange dream he had about a creature which looked like Seegook's "Seagod."

"Do you know yet what happened to you when you sort of went faint, or whatever it was?" Holly asked.

"No, I still can't quite figure it out. It just seemed I flew out of my body," David said. He paused, then added, "Seegook's art must have had quite an impact on me to keep me seeing it all night. I am certainly intrigued by those humanoid figures. Seegook's comments about his uncle, and your contribution about the same basic images and signs in different cultures were so fascinating."

Holly answered thoughtfully, "Yes, it is interesting how the same motifs are used by humans all over the world. It seems like so many of the world's cultures have similar historical backgrounds. In your mother's art classes, I was fascinated by the recurrence of symbols like the "tree of life" or the "praying or blessing figure" like Seegook uses so often. I've seen them in embroideries from Eastern Europe to South America. They show up in ancient cultures, too. To me, it just shows we are all human and have similar experiences, needs, and desires no matter what culture we come from."

David sat deep in thought as he sipped an after dinner coffee. "Think all those common motifs show we've been visited before?"

Holly answered, "You mean, like the theories about aliens building the pyramids? No, I don't think so."

They often had fun arguing over questions with no answers, but David did not feel like playing tonight. Too much had happened in the past two days. He sat, quietly thinking about the meeting with Ward, and watching Holly wash the dinner dishes. He wished he could confide in her, tell her the fears he had about this assignment. In one way, it was exciting to think he would be doing something which could turn out to be historically important. On the other hand, he knew it was dangerous. What would happen to Holly if he didn't come back? Would they tell her the truth?

He wondered about his family, too. He hadn't even called to tell them good-bye. Feeling a little guilty for having forgotten something so important, he dialed their number. They weren't home.

"Hi Mom," he told the recorder. "I'm going to be gone a few days, but I'll give you a call when I get home. Holly has the pets. Anyway, sorry I missed you." He started to hang up, then added, "I love you all." He realized this might seem strange, and hoped it didn't sound like a last call.

Holly started to ask who he was talking to when his cell phone rang.

"David, this is Ward," the voice sounded strained.

"Hi," David answered, almost in a whisper.

"Everything is set. You will be contacted at your hotel about where to meet the man who will give you your credentials," Ward said.

"Is there anything else I need to know right now?" David asked.

"Just to be on your guard. We don't know who else knows about this. You've got to be careful, and don't trust anyone."

"How about the man with my credentials?" David asked.

"Don't trust anyone too far, but I think he's good. I think there might be some of the Indians involved with this, too. My contact says they've just learned they might be able to help. Could help with your cover."

"Is there anyone in particular I should contact?" David whispered.

"They said you'll know all you need to know at the right time. I guess you are supposed to sit tight and wait. Good luck, David," Ward said.

"Don't worry, Ward. I'll see you soon," David tried to put Ward at ease, even as he felt more tense.

"Who was that?" Holly asked, her back turned to David as she continued working over the kitchen sink.

"Just Ward, giving me details about the trip tomorrow," David tried to keep his voice from cracking with emotion.

Holly continued to hum, unaware of David's struggle to leave her, knowing he might never see her again.

Chapter 6

The morning came too early. Running late, as usual, David hurriedly finished packing with a piece of toast in hand. Gulping down the cup of coffee Holly brought to him, David noted Bastet's uneasy manner and tried to comfort her. She always seemed to sense when he was leaving. The bird chattered away, and for a brief moment, David was overwhelmed by the wonder of animal intuition seemingly so much sharper than human awareness of events.

Holly's voice interrupted his silent conversation with Bastet and the chirping bird.

"David, it's getting late. Are you ready to go? We have to go if you hope to make your flight. I have to stop for gas, too."

She appeared at the kitchen doorway with another slice of toast as a peace offering to compensate for the news she had just conveyed to David.

"What do you mean, you need gas? We should have stopped at the station last night." David's voice sounded like he was annoyed by her oversight, but he was just uneasy about the trip.

Holly apologized for her forgetfulness. "I didn't think of it because I was just trying to get over here after sailing and get dinner on time. Anyway, it's too late to argue about it now. We can stop at the station on the corner."

"Ok, let's go then," David said, as he put the cat down. He walked to the bird's cage and stuck his finger in to stroke the bird's feathers as a kind of good-bye gesture. Icarus jumped up on David's fingers and chirped.

David spoke to the bird. "See you soon. Be good for Holly."

Holly picked up David's case and David made a final visual check of the house as he closed and locked the door. Holly was already in the car when David reached it. He looked over at the gas gauge, then at Holly who wryly noted, "It's only on empty. Maybe we can make it."

David rolled his eyes and they pulled onto the street. Fortunately, there was no line at the station. David jumped out to pump the gas while Holly went into the station to pay. The freeways were clear as it was early on Sunday morning. They made good time to the airport. Holly dropped him off at the gate. David took his bag from the car as Holly promised to join him after parking.

David headed to the check-in counter where he was told to pick up his ticket. The clerk brought his ticket after checking the reservation, and told him, "We also have a message for you, sir. Mr. Ward Brass called to say the person you are to meet has had a change of plans. He cannot meet you tonight, but will call at your hotel to tell you where the two of you can get together tomorrow. He also said to have a good trip."

The agent smiled at the last part of the message. She handed the ticket to him as she explained the particulars of his flight.

Holly came up behind him. "Problems with the ticket, dear?" "No, it's all ok," David answered her. "It looks like I have to go through Salt Lake and take one of those little milk runs."

Holly was not a good traveler. She avoided flying whenever it was possible. She claimed flying made her claustrophobic, and for this reason, she always tried to get window seats. At least, she could see out. Whenever David flew someplace with Holly, he noticed how her palms would sweat. In turbulence, Holly would close her eyes and hang onto her arm rests so tightly her knuckles turned white. There was much truth in the description of those afraid to fly as "white-knuckle flyers." Holly was living proof.

David heard her comment on his flight.

"It will probably be a bumpy flight, even if the weather is good. I hate those things."

"I don't have any option. You know, beggars can't be choosers," David said.

"What an original saying," Holly said as she squeezed his arm and smiled at him.

David answered as they turned to leave the counter, "Don't be catty, sweetie. Let's get down to the gate."

David picked up his case with his free hand and the two of them walked hand in hand to the security clearance gate. He placed his case on the ramp for the x-ray and walked through the gate without incident, and down the concourse towards the gate. They sat quietly together at the gate, sipping coffee. David was deep in thought.

"What are you thinking about?" Holly asked him, still concerned about David's recent experience and the effect it seemed to have on his mood.

"The person I was supposed to meet today contacted Ward and can't make it until tomorrow," David said, puzzled.

"How did you find that out?" Holly asked.

"Before you got back from parking the car, the ticket agent gave me a message from Ward. I guess he called here to leave it this morning." David's brow was furrowed and Holly sensed his bewilderment. David continued, "I was just wondering what was going on and why there was the change in plan. I guess I'll find out when I get there."

Holly squeezed his hand to reassure him all would be fine.

The gate agent switched on the intercom and gave the boarding announcement. David stood in line to board the flight, gave Holly a kiss, and promised to call when he arrived at his hotel.

He was directed to his seat by the uniformed flight attendant at the door, and placed his bag in the bin above the seat. David apologized to the smartly-dressed man in the aisle seat of his row, as he struggled to climb over the man's feet to get to the window seat.

David looked towards the terminal as they pulled away. The plane taxied out for what seemed miles to the runway, and stopped at the end of the tarmac. The engines started to whine and David felt himself pulled back into the seat as the plane began to increase in power and speed. About half-way down the runway, he felt the wheels leave the ground, and he could see the shadows of the tires as they lifted off the runway.

Flight is an amazing thing, David thought. How an aircraft so large and heavy could rise from the earth with such ease seemed impossible. David could understand why there had always been such a fascination with flight and with the freedom of birds. From Daedalus and Icarus of the Greeks to Da Vinci, and his flying machines, to the Apollo moon program, man has always been preoccupied with flight.

The plane reached its cruising altitude, and David pushed back his seat to gaze out the window. The day was glorious. The sun had risen not long before and cast long shadows through the white, billowy clouds, giving stark contrast to the blue sky. Below, the distance to the earth grew ever greater, and David noted the wonderful patterns of the city blocks, curved suburban cul-de-sacs, and freeways. Somehow, city planning looked better from the air than it did from the ground. Even the air over the city was good today, without as much haze as usual for LA.

The attendant brought breakfast, and as David ate he continued to watch the sights beneath him. By now, the city had been left far behind, but patterns on the earth below were like a patchwork quilt. The mountains seemed so much smaller than when he had driven through them. They were like crinkled paper instead of majestic peaks. The deserts, too, were gouged with stream beds and canyons giving them a much different look than one would notice from the ground.

The angle of the sun played with the desert formations and cast shadows making different colors appear — first red, then yellow, then orange, then brown. Most vibrant were the patterns of green. The majority of these were not natural to this dry desert land, but the result of human intervention.

David thought the fields divided into squares and rectangles were beautiful, but even more stunning were the circles where irrigated patches resulted from sprinklers turning from a center point. Dozens of green circles dotted the red and brown landscape.

David smiled as he thought of the irony of language. These were real "crop circles." They were without doubt made by intelligent life!

His thoughts wandered to the stories he had read not long ago about the upsurge in the other kind of crop circles — those strange, inexplicable patterns found in corn and wheat fields in England, France, Canada, the United States, and elsewhere in the world. Some of them were also of great beauty, and seem to have been the result of some kind of intelligent plan instead of natural forces, just as these irrigation patterns stood out from the desert.

David thought aliens, if they existed and came near the earth, would recognize these irrigated crazy quilt and polka-dot patterns as evidence of life on earth. Maybe they would interpret them as deliberate messages.

David wondered if it could be possible the other, mysterious crop circles were signals left by aliens, but humans just did not know how to translate these hieroglyphs yet.

"You have a beautiful ring there," David heard the man next to him say. He resented the intrusion, and didn't feel like talking. Yet, he found himself explaining how he came to wear it. A present from Holly, it was a large silver and turquoise treasure which took up almost half his finger — a stunning piece of Navajo art, and he often received comments about it.

"It's Navajo, isn't it?" the man observed. "It's of very good quality and design."

David was surprised that the man recognized the work, and became more interested in a conversation with him.

"How do you know about Indian jewelry," David inquired.

The man smiled. "It's been a hobby of mine," he answered. "I'm not just interested in Native American art and culture."

"Oh?" David asked with growing interest.

"In fact, I'm just on my way back from a trip to Australia."

"Really? What were you doing there?" David shifted in his seat and examined the clothing and manner of the man beside him. He wondered what this man did for a living — he certainly seemed to do well at whatever it was. His fashionable elegance gave the impression of a man who knew and enjoyed the finest things in life, and many opportunities to indulge in them wherever he liked. Yet, he did not seem to answer David's simplest questions with direct answers.

"You know, in Australia, the Aborigines have developed forms of art with deep and often secret meanings," the man started to lecture him. David wasn't sure how his own ring had led to a speech about Australian Aboriginal art, but as he was interested in the topic, he didn't care. He was happy to listen instead of talk anyway, but interjected, "I was at an art gallery the other night that had some Aboriginal art. I wish I knew more about it."

"Most of what you see today refers back to original themes, but the secret paintings are not shown to those who are not properly initiated. You see, the art is invested with great power. It is dangerous to those who have not undergone initiation. There are those who still believe that desecration, by women, by outsiders, by the uninitiated will cause destruction that can only be redressed by punishment of the offender," the man continued without telling David how he came by his information.

"What kind of punishment," David asked.

"Death," the man answered simply.

"Surely not," David voiced his doubt. "There must be laws against killing people for looking at art."

"It's not for looking at art. It's for desecration of tribal laws. This is critical to the continuance of the universe. The Law is what keeps the universe going, and when it is disrupted..." the man's voice trailed off without finishing the thought.

"But they sell this art. It's a commodity," David pointed out.

"No. Most of what is sold may be allowable, but it is not real art in a certain sense," the man explained.

"What do you mean, not real art?" David asked.

"Real art is a way of showing the spirit world," he continued. "The artist is able to transform in a visual way what is given from a spiritual source. This is true whether the depiction comes from Aboriginal Australia, from Native America, from Siberia, from the ancient Egyptians, or for that matter, from Medieval Christian Europe," he declared. "The art of all these cultures makes visible the unseen spiritual world."

David was mesmerized by this stranger. He spoke with authority and confidence which comes from a long education and wide range of life experiences. "Don't you think it's a bit of stretch to compare aboriginal art to European?" he asked.

"In each case, the art is a window into an unseen universe. You may disagree with the ritual or even with the depiction, but the fact remains that true art is religious — it shows us the spirit world whether we want to see it or not."

David recalled Seegook's "Seagod" and the powerful experience he had at the gallery. He heard the man's voice continue, "If you concentrate on art that is real, you'll find yourself drawn into the spiritual meaning behind the exterior style or form of the thing. You will not be able to help yourself. Art, in whatever form — painting, sculpture, writing — plants an image or psyche in the observer. If this is accomplished, then art has achieved its purpose."

David realized with a shock that the flight was almost over. He gazed out the window and felt the familiar pattern of descent as the wheels bumped against the runway, but felt an unfamiliar sense of mystery as he thought about his companion's philosophy and his own disturbing yet exciting experience. He never did find out who the man was or what he did. David turned to ask the man, but he was not there. David looked for him in the crowd, and saw him. It appeared that the man began to fade away as if he never existed. David almost wondered if he had dreamed the whole encounter, or if the man had simply walked into a painting.

Chapter 7

David blocked the strange man from his thoughts and moved through the terminal, looking for a screen to tell him where commuter flight 7055 to Rapid City departed.

"Great," he said aloud to no one in particular, trying to regain a sense of the normal. "It would have to be at the opposite end of the terminal."

Annoyed at the prospect of carrying his bag from one end of the terminal to the other, he set out at a quick pace. He hoped he would not miss his flight because he could not get across the terminal in time. His flight had already boarded by the time he arrived at the gate. Breathless, he handed his pass to the attendant who rushed him onto the plane.

The flight was uneventful, but crowded. Next to David, a salesman kept up a running one-sided conversation with him. David was courteous, but a little resentful he could not spend more time watching the patterns of the clouds out the window. His quiet mood had returned.

The flight never reached the elevation of the previous jet, so the circles and squares on the ground were less distinct. David longed for silence. He wondered if the salesman was a nervous flyer. Some people find talking gives them a way to cope with their fear of flying.

The flight was bumpy, and this fact probably contributed to the nervous chatter of David's seat mate. Between comments, David gazed at the puffy white clouds, through which the plane darted as if playing hide and seek.

David had an overwhelming desire to jump out the plane's window and roll around on the soft surface of the clouds. They looked solid enough, like huge cotton balls or great snowdrifts.

His mind wandered back to Seegook and the stories of shamans flying above the earth, unconstrained by metal aircraft walls and glass windows, free as the birds soaring on the currents of air. David thought flying like a bird would be liberating. He decided to read again the books on flying shamans.

After his flight landed, David headed to the exit to hail a taxi. He glanced up in surprise when he heard his name announced by the intercom page. David picked up the paging telephone, but the message he heard made no sense to him. Its content was mysterious, and the sender was anonymous.

The message attendant read to David, "We know you have arrived to meet with your contact. We will be watching you."

David could not make out what the message at the airport meant. He puzzled over it as he rode in the cab to his hotel, but could not figure out who had left it, or why. He paid the fare and took his bag to the reception desk of the hotel to check in.

"Welcome to Rapid City, Mr. Seabird." The cheerful, pleasant voice belonged to the girl at the counter. David completed his registration as the young lady engaged in small talk.

"Are you Native American? You know, we have so many different names in this part of the country."

David responded, "No, it's not a Native American name, but I hope people will think it is while I'm here." He chuckled, and she smiled broadly.

"You are in room 325. Here is your key. You will find the elevator down the hallway to your right," she explained as she pointed the direction David should follow.

David was soon settled in a comfortable and cheery room. He dialed his home number hoping to reach Holly. He reached the answering machine and left the message that he had arrived safely and gave his room number. He hung up the receiver, disappointed he had not been able to hear Holly's voice.

He looked at the room service menu and decided to find a restaurant near the hotel instead. David had gone no further than the door when the telephone rang. He lunged toward the phone, anticipating Holly's voice at the other end of the line.

"Hello." David almost shouted the greeting, somewhat breathless from rushing across the room.

The voice was not Holly's. It was cold and deep.

"I will meet you tomorrow at the Mount Rushmore visitors' center at 2:00 p.m. I know what you look like and will find you then." The line went dead.

David clicked the phone and repeatedly said "Hello" trying to raise a response from the caller. It was no use. David replaced the receiver in its cradle and sat on the edge of the bed in bewilderment. This was the second strange call of the day. He could not make out if this most recent message was from the person he was supposed to meet, or from the same person who left the page at the airport.

He considered calling Ward, but decided whatever he might have to say would sound like a case of paranoia. He would wait until tomorrow. He could call Ward then, and at least have something to report.

David's thoughts were interrupted by the shrill ringing of the telephone beside the bed. He jumped, startled by the noise. He considered not answering it at all, but instead raised the receiver to his ear and listened for a voice at the other end.

There was at first only silence. David heard Holly's voice asking, "Hello? Is anyone there?"

David felt his heart pounding. "Holly, I'm glad it is you."

There was an air of bewilderment in Holly's answer to him. "Who else did you think it would be?"

David did not answer her question, but just said, "I tried to call you a few minutes ago." He realized he could not tell her anything else. He was happy to have a change in topic and stretched out on the bed as he talked, trying to convince himself to relax.

David and Holly continued to visit for a long time about nothing in particular. He told her about his flight, and she told him about her day. They talked about the pets, the weather, and whatever else came to mind.

It merely took hearing Holly's voice to raise David's spirits. The eerie feeling left by the earlier call was dispelled by the time

David finished the conversation with Holly. He left his room feeling cheerful once more, walked to the front desk, and asked for a restaurant recommendation.

The same girl who had been interested in David's name was only too happy to visit with him again. She gave him a few recommendations for nearby restaurants.

"Since you said you wanted people to think you were an Indian while you were here, you might want to go to the Indian bar just down the street. It's the best place here for local color," she said as she pointed out the direction.

David thanked her with a smile and headed out the door to the restaurant she had recommended. Refreshed by his meal, David decided the evening was young, especially since he was still on California time. This was a good time to experience the local atmosphere. He turned down the street, entered the bar suggested by the clerk, and found it to be all she had promised.

David's eyes adjusted to the dark, smoky room. He wandered up to the bar and sat at the counter next to several Indians. The background music blared as a local band played old Eagles tunes. Several couples swayed to the music in the space in front of the band which served as a dance floor.

"What'll you have?" The old bartender asked for David's order. He was a grizzled, tough looking man and David had no doubt he could double as the bouncer.

David ordered a beer, and looked around the bar as he waited for it to be served to him. He felt oddly comfortable in this unfamiliar environment. David was surprised by his sense of ease, for he would have expected to feel more like a stranger here.

The lead singer of the band wailed a decent version of "Desperado." David watched the couples on the dance floor enjoying the music. The words of the song seemed to fit some of the characters seated at the tables of the smoke-filled room. Most seemed oblivious to the music, or to anything but their loud conversations. This was no quiet lounge where businessmen struck deals over fancy cocktails. It was the Wild West — lively, noisy, grungy.

The bartender brought David's beer. David took a sip. He glanced up to look over the rim of his glass and noticed the man seated next to him.

The man's hair was in two long braids. He wore a beaded bone choker and red shirt. His striking appearance was enhanced by his height and dignified bearing. David felt the Indian's stare.

"Hey, washeechoo, where did you get the ring? Brothers from the southwest?" The Indian's deep, velvety voice matched his regal appearance.

David glanced at the ring, and back to the man.

"My girlfriend gave it to me," David explained as he held up his hand. "It was from a Navajo friend of hers."

"I'd like to meet your girlfriend." The man did not smile or show any emotion, and David was not sure what the man meant. The man could see his droll manner had the desired effect of confusing David. He flashed a smile and extended his hand in greeting to David as he introduced himself. "I'm Dale Spirit Wolf."

"David Seabird," David shook his hand as he returned the introduction.

Dale took a sip of beer and continued the conversation. "What tribe are you?"

"Wannabee, I guess," David answered as he looked down at the counter, a little embarrassed. He did not know how Dale would react to his own subtle humor.

Dale broke into a peal of laughter. He paused and said, "Hey, some of my best friends are Wannabees! Most of them won't admit it though. They claim they are 'real Indians' like me."

Both men paused for another drink from their glasses. Dale asked, "How did you get a name like Seabird? It sounds like it should belong to an Indian."

David explained to Dale, "When my great-grandfather immigrated here, his name was Sieberg. The immigration officer recorded it wrong and put down Seabird. So we've been Seabirds ever since."

Dale laughed before he said, "The immigration officer must have been an Indian—didn't know English yet."

David was not sure if Dale was being facetious or serious. Dale continued, "Yeah, all our problems started with your great-grandfathers immigrating over here."

David recognized it was a statement of fact, not a personal indictment against him in particular.

David did not want any unfriendly conversations and changed the subject by asking Dale, "What tribe are you? Sioux?"

Dale answered with pride, "The great Sioux Nation, Oglala Lakota."

"Have you lived here all your life?" David continued with small-talk.

"Since the earth was created," Dale answered in tones connoting deep and serious wisdom.

David did not understand. He was uncertain if Dale was serious or merely pulling his leg as a white man. David did not know what to say, he forgot his earlier resolve to avoid controversial issues and asked, "What did you mean about all your problems starting with my great-grandfather?"

"Our troubles started with our first contact with the white man. The beginning of contact was the beginning of the BIA. The BIA is nothin' but damn bureaucratic foul-ups, submissive regulations, and government control of our lives. Basically Communist, you know."

David thought Dale was joking. "Yeah, right," he said.

"No, really." Dale answered. "Communism is a government-controlled political system. Everything the Communists do is done for the good of the government. It's a communal society. Just like reservations. They are run by the government, too. We are actually just like little Communist societies here on the reservation, don't you think?"

"I guess so," David was still trying to figure out what Dale was saying.

"Our government was so busy chasing after Communists in Hollywood and under every other rock, they didn't even know they were creating little communist enclaves right in their own backyards. Reagan was so intent on bringing down the 'Evil Empire,' he forgot to look at what the government had already created for us Indians in this country." Dale said lifting his glass for a sip.

"You know what BIA means, don't you?" Dale asked.

For the first time, David sensed a genuine bitterness in Dale's speech. He gave the obvious answer for the government agency's acronym, "Bureau of Indian Affairs."

Dale did not look at David, but took a drink before answering. He stared straight ahead as he said, "Wrong, brother." Dale turned, looked at David, and continued in a more humorous tone, "It means 'Boss Indians Around.' 'Burro of Indian Affairs.' 'Bureaucratic Intrusive Affairs.' 'Bureau of Incompetent Asses.' I could tell you lots more, but they aren't so complimentary. Know what I mean?"

David was aware many Indians had a deep sense of mistrust about the agency created to be their advocate in the federal government. This was the first time he heard anyone express the bitterness with such mockery.

David spoke, "It doesn't sound like you think much of the BIA."

Dale shot back, "Hey, man, if you knew how they screwed up life here, you wouldn't think much of them either."

David could see Dale's strong emotions as Dale gave examples of the long history of tensions between the Sioux and the government.

"Take the Black Hills, our Sacred Grounds. They tried to take it away from us, then gave it to us by treaty. They bungled that. They found gold and it was something they wanted, so they lied to us and broke the treaties."

David had read about the problem with the Black Hills and knew it was a sensitive issue. Dale continued, "They tried to destroy our culture and language by shipping us off to boarding schools and forbidding us to speak in our own languages. All they had to do was split up our families and our tribes. They could destroy us by assimilation. They tried to turn us into White Indians. Have you ever heard of Apple Indians?"

David confessed he had not. Dale said, "Red on the outside, but white on the Inside. That's assimilation. Our people used to call them, 'Hang around the fort Indians.' They just want to be like you whites."

David looked down at his glass. It was nearly empty. He did not know what to say to Dale, but he did not feel comfortable with the facts of his culture's treatment of Indians pointed out by Dale.

"How about another beer?" David offered. Dale accepted. David flagged the bartender and gave him the order, then asked Dale to continue.

"The government gave us reservations then tried to keep us in poverty on them. They give us second class medical care which they call the Indian Health Service. BIA schools don't get many resources but they do get lots of teachers that don't care about our ways. Some of them are only paying off their retirement houses in Oregon."

"Why Oregon?" David could not make the connection between BIA schools and the leap to retirement homes in Oregon.

Dale laughed wryly, then explained with sarcasm, "It's where all the rednecks retire together so they can talk about what great things they did for us Indians while they enjoy a mild climate and nice beaches."

Dale paused as the bartender brought the beers, then continued, "They say if we're still poor and unhealthy and uneducated, it's 'cause we aren't grateful enough for their paternalistic help."

Dale and David sipped their beers in silence. Both turned and listened to the band blaring. A few minutes passed, then Dale turned back to David and asked, "Are you another of the bureaucrats come to save us?"

David smiled and shook his head.

"No," he said, "I'm just a journalist."

Dale looked a little suspicious, cocked his head to the side, and asked, "One of those who writes about the bad conditions here, eh?"

David answered, "I'm not out here on any assignments about reservations, if that's what you mean. It sounds like you could use some press to shake things up, though."

Dale replied, "When we get press, it's usually bad. It always comes out sounding like we are to blame for whatever is wrong here. Things don't usually get better. Not even Robert Kennedy could make things better, but he at least tried."

David steered the conversation back to the present.

"I'm working on a story here. I wish I could meet an Indian man I read about."

Dale glanced up from his beer and asked, "What's the man's name?"

David answered, "Someone called Sam Going Away."

David saw Dale's face soften and take on a friendlier expression.

Dale smiled and sipped his beer. He almost drawled as he said, "Ole Sam. What do you want with him?"

David was surprised at the possibility Dale knew the man he hoped to meet.

"Do you know Sam Going Away?"

Dale said, "Who around here doesn't know him?"

David returned to Dale's earlier question of David's interest in the old man.

"I read a story about a person who had been found wandering around up in this area. Sam Going Away had taken him in and helped him. I was interested in a man who was kind to others. I am also interested in the question of jurisdiction over tribal lands."

Dale looked at David with a better understanding of the journalist's motivations and depth of character. He decided he liked David. Dale answered, "Yeah, Sam is a kind man. He's a wise man. Sam knows when to back away from fights and when to stand up for what is right. He makes good medicine. Some uppity Indians who aren't from here think he's old fashioned or crazy, but he's wise and he's powerful."

"What do you mean, powerful?" David asked with increasing interest in the old man.

"He has power beyond what people like you or me will ever understand. He can fly. He can talk to animal spirits. He can heal people. He has strong medicine." Dale's eyes glistened in the dim light and they seemed to be seeing something far away. David could no longer hear the noise and music in the bar. He felt like the two of them were in a world separate from everything around them. David spoke, already anticipating the answer to his question, and recalling the image of Seegook's Seagod in his mind.

"You mean he travels around the country giving seminars or something?"

"No, he can fly," replied Dale in what seemed like a whisper. "He doesn't need a white man's plane. He knows how to fly like the birds, like all those with strong medicine could long before white men were ever making metal planes."

"How do you know he can fly by himself?" David was entranced by Dale's statement and the respect he conveyed for the old man's abilities.

"He's told me. I've seen him do all kinds of things." Dale paused. "I've been in the sweathouse with him where his spiritual medicine is strongest. I can't explain it. I only know what he told me is true."

David had read about the importance of sweathouses, and was aware claims of medical healing, foretelling the future, and other unexplained phenomena were associated with sweathouses.

David's genuine interest was apparent to Dale, who told David more stories from the fantastic to the historic. The conversation was punctuated by interruptions as Dale's friends and acquaintances greeted Dale and met David.

"Last call," the bartender sang out in his raspy voice.

"Already?" said David, who had lost all track of time.

David was amazed to discover that it was 1:00 a.m. He had learned much about the history and culture of the area and regretted seeing the evening come to a close.

Dale and David left the bar, and before they parted company, Dale paid David a great compliment.

"You're ok. You're not like most white men. Maybe your name does make you a real Indian. You have a good spirit like an Indian." Dale paused, then shook David's hand in parting.

"Would you like me to take you to Sam Going Away?" he asked.

"Would you?" David felt his pulse rush with excitement.

"Yeah, I will," promised Dale. "When do you want to go?"

"I have an appointment tomorrow. How about the next day?" David was almost willing to skip his meeting for a chance like this.

"I'll pick you up the day after tomorrow, about 10 or so, yeah? Plan to be gone all day," Dale instructed.

David said trying to hide his excitement, "Great. I'll see you then."

David returned to the hotel. He had already forgotten the cloud brought on by the earlier mysterious messages. He felt exhilaration about the coming meeting with Sam Going Away, and an inner warmth from the conversation with Dale.

He walked past the reception desk and asked the clerk to check for messages.

"Yes, sir, Mr. Seabird," the young man at the desk came back with a manila envelope. "We have an envelope for you left earlier this evening. Good night, sir."

He wasn't expecting any envelope. He stepped into his room and opened it. A key fell out and landed by his foot. A small piece of paper had a cryptic typed message: "In case unexpected events prevent our meeting, I have left information for you in a security box 11357, in the Bank of Gallup, Gallup, New Mexico. P. Rosenburg."

The note slipped from David's trembling hand.

Chapter 8

David made his way to the entrance of the Mount Rushmore Visitors' Center. The last few hours had been troubled ones, and he hoped to soon put this assignment behind him. He did not like the way it was developing. The one bright spot was the anticipation of his meeting with Sam Going Away. He would have to wait until tomorrow for the more pleasant part of this job.

He glanced around the crowd, trying to pick out who among them might be his contact.

"Look at these clones in polyester shorts." David heard the grating voice of a large, pushy woman commenting to her weedy little husband. "They all look like they're straight out of Nebraska," she continued caustically as she shoved her way past David to reach the head of the line. Her little husband, himself clad in polyester shorts, obediently followed, giving David a pathetic look of apology for his wife's behavior.

David did not know who he was looking for. Clones, indeed. Everyone seemed alike, wearing T-shirts advertising homes and vacation destinations, sun hats, and cameras.

He spotted a few foreign tourists in the crowd, but was he looking for someone foreign. He did not know. He would simply have to wait for his contact to find him.

"Scusa," a woman with a Italian accent was speaking to him. Maybe she was the one. But instead, she merely asked, "Why did they not put the face of the other Roosevelt on the wall?"

"I'm sorry, ma'am, but I don't know. Maybe you should ask one of the guides over there." He pointed out a ranger, a bit annoyed that this had led him no closer to finding out why he was here.

He watched as a guide with a large umbrella herded along a group of Japanese tourists. They crowded past him as the guide rushed through a hasty explanation of something or other about the site, and scurried the group along to the next point of interest.

Killing time, he wandered over to the coffee shop and ordered an ice cream. "How long am I supposed to wait?" he wondered to himself.

He moved toward one of the lookouts, still watching for someone watching him. Suddenly, he heard a woman's piercing scream. "O my God, someone come here!" Someone else yelled as David noticed a commotion near the edge of a cliff by a lookout point.

The gathering crowd jumbled together in agitation, jostling against one another for the best vantage point.

"Someone's fallen over — get an ambulance!" A voice yelled the command.

A man pushed past him as he ran toward the Tourist Center. David joined the river of bodies moving in the direction of the cliff edge. He could see nothing. The crowd continued to press in around him. He felt choked by claustrophobia. David struggled against the flow, gasping for air. He stumbled as he pushed through the last line of assembled on-lookers, in time to see the rescue crew arrive.

It seemed to David to have taken forever for the park rangers and medical rescue team to appear. The rescue team scaled the precipice over which the person had fallen as the rangers moved the crowd away and began setting up barriers. David stood away from the assembled crowd of the curious, grateful to feel able to breathe again. He watched as the body was hoisted to the ledge and could see the unfortunate man was perhaps in his late forties and slightly balding.

David could not help feeling an eerie sense of foreboding. He wondered if this accident was related to the mysterious messages he had received the previous day. He watched the crowd move about the site of the accident, then disperse into little groups conversing in silent whispers.

His contact did not seem to be present. David was not sure if the man had been here at all. David went over the instructions in his mind. All he was supposed to do was show up. The man said he would find him. David moved to a bench, sat down and hoped the mysterious man would make himself known.

The body was eventually taken away. The crowd buzzed in hushed whispers. David sensed the change in atmosphere as the holiday mood was replaced by one of curiosity, sadness, and tragedy meted out by Fate.

No one seemed to know what had happened. David could hear among the murmurs that the man had jumped. Others said he had slipped while stepping over a rail. One man swore he saw the man get pushed by another who disappeared into the crowd. David's spirits sank.

David waited as long as possible for his contact to join him. The park was declared closed because of the accident, however, and David had no choice but to join the masses of tourists leaving the center. He kept looking for someone who might be seeking him out. David had a sense of dread that someone else had found his contact first.

When he returned to his room, he checked his messages. Maybe the man never got to the park at all. There could be a note or call waiting for David saying that the man missed the meeting and wanted to rearrange a time to get together.

There were no messages for David. He entered his room and sat on the bed, thinking about the past two days. He did not like any of this at all. David's palms were sweaty. His heart was beating so hard he could hear the thumping in his head.

He pulled out the note he had received with the key the previous evening, and decided he should at least let Ward know what was going on.

David was startled by the ringing of the phone.

"Hello," David said. He hoped it would be the man he was supposed to meet. Instead, it was one he had never heard before. A voice accented by a heavy Southern drawl said, "Your contact had a little accident. We're watchin' you, so watch yourself. Keep your nose out of othuh people's business if ya don't wanna lose it. Git my jist?"

Chapter 9

The line went dead. David held the receiver, stunned and shaken. Now, he was almost certain that his contact was the man who had gone off the side of the cliff.

If the dead man was the one he was going to meet, someone else knew about it. Maybe the person who just called him was the same one seen by the eyewitness who claimed the dead man had been pushed off the cliff.

His contact had been watched, and it was possible the same people were watching him, too. It was obvious, in fact, when they ended their messages to him with warnings to watch his step.

David had no idea where his steps were taking him. How could he watch them? He toyed with the idea of checking out and taking the next flight home.

Instead, he left his room and went down the street to the Indian bar. He had noticed a pay phone there the previous evening. Maybe he was being paranoid, but David decided not to use the phone in his room to call Ward. He wanted to talk in private, without any uninvited listeners. David dialed Ward's number.

"Ward Brass." David felt relief when he heard Ward's smooth, confident voice.

"Hi, Ward. It's David." David tried not to sound upset, but could feel the words choke through his constricted throat.

"David, I'm glad to hear from you. Were you able to find out anything?" Ward asked.

David was almost certain Ward's voice had taken on a slight edge, as if he sensed David's distress.

"I'm at a pay phone because I wasn't sure my hotel phone was safe," David blurted out.

"What has happened?" Ward asked with concern.

"My contact never showed up. I went up to the Visitors' Center to meet him as arranged, but never saw him. He ended up at the bottom of the cliff. I've had another warning to lay off."

David switched the receiver to his other hand and wiped the sweat from his palm onto his pants.

"What makes you so sure he was killed?" Ward's interest was tempered by concern for David's safety.

"Someone got pushed off. And I've received some strange messages since I arrived. First, someone paged me at the airport. No one but you and I knew I would be there. The same people called again at the hotel after I returned today."

"What did they tell you?" Ward asked.

"They said I should keep my nose out of other people's business if I expect to keep it," David paraphrased the warning he had just received.

"They sound like a nice bunch," Ward's voice reflected the irony of his statement. "Anything else?"

David continued, "The man I was supposed to contact left an envelope for me at the front desk last night. I think he knew we might not be able to meet. Seems he made a contingency plan."

"Was there anything else in it?" Ward asked.

"Yeah," David said. "A key to a safety deposit box in Gallup. I think it must have documents that might shed a little light on all this. Did you know this guy?"

"I dunno. I haven't heard from my own contacts since I met with you. I wonder why he wants you to go to Gallup." Ward was puzzled by the seeming lack of connections between New Mexico and South Dakota. "Suppose this has to do with the theory that there is another center down there?"

"Maybe. Guess the only way we'll know is if I go down there and find out." David admitted.

"This sounds strange," Ward said. "Let me get ahold of my source in D.C. and see if I can get any confirmation about your theory on the 'accident'." David was glad to transfer some of the burden he felt onto Ward's shoulders.

Ward asked, "Can you hang on there a day or two?"

"Sure," David answered.

"Are you going to be able to check out the secret installation without having met your contact?" Ward asked almost as an afterthought.

"I dunno. I haven't really made any other inquiries. Thought I might find out all I needed today. Guess there's no chance of that. You want me to see what I can do in the meantime, then?"

"Yeah, New Mexico can wait a few days." Ward directed.

"Ok," said Ward. "I'll get in touch with you soon, and I'll see what we can do to get this cleared up. Be careful and watch your back. Try and call every day to let me know you're still with us."

"That's a nice way to put it." David felt a sense of relief, and laughed at Ward's attempt at humor in the face of uncertainty. "I'll call when I can," he promised.

"Good. Take care," Ward said in a commanding voice.

"Thanks," David said as he hung up the phone.

David walked back to his hotel. He didn't feel much like talking to anyone and was glad to get back to the privacy of his room.

The events of the past two days had shaken him. He was certain his contact was the same man he had seen lying at the bottom of the cliff. Why was he killed?

David knew suicide was not the cause. It did not make sense. A man would not go to the effort to contact a journalist from half way across the country, then jump off the cliff moments before they were supposed to meet.

It might have been an accident, but David doubted it. Accidents are usually the result of adventurers taking chances, kids wandering too close to barriers, or climbing over them. Someone choosing a populated place to meet a journalist would have little interest in the sites. Lookouts are safe unless one teeters on the edge, tempting fate.

If the man was his contact, only murder made sense. What was it he knew? Why would someone want him dead?

David looked at the note and key from the envelope he had received the night before. He shuddered as he remembered today's phone call and the airport page. He was reminded he was being watched, perhaps by the same man who had killed his contact. Did the killer know David had been warned about the contact's death?

He was scared, and excited, too. This was the kind of assignment he had wanted as a journalist. It gave him an adrenaline rush and sharpened his senses. He had to solve the mystery, regardless of the cost.

The shrill ring of the phone made him jump.

David reluctantly lifted the receiver and spoke.

"Hello," he said quietly, expecting to hear another mysterious male voice.

"Hi, David?" It was Holly's cheery greeting. David was relieved. The fact he had not expected the call to be from Holly made him all the happier that it was her.

"How did the day go?" She asked innocently.

"It's been interesting," David decided this much was not a lie. He tried to sound carefree. "I've been running from one place to the next, following up the regular leads."

David smiled at the absurdity of his answer to her. He could say he had no idea why he was there in the first place. He had seen a guy die. He might be next. It was quite a day to tell a girlfriend about. Instead of impressing her with the truth, he lied.

"How's the assignment going?" Holly asked.

"I'm hoping for a story tomorrow. I'm trying to fit the pieces together." David said.

"What pieces?" Holly asked.

"Pieces about Indians. You know, 'Peace' and 'Indians'?" David was glad to have something take his mind away from the real assignment, and grateful for Holly's call.

"I think you made up something so you could go up there to meet some Indians. You know, do more 'research'," Holly accused him in jest. Her voice became serious. "You seem stressed. You ok? You're probably still thinking about the art show we went to the other night, aren't you, and your weird experience."

"Yeah, you're right. Can't hide anything from you, can I. No, really, I'm fine. I met a guy named Dale Spirit Wolf. He's a Lakota Sioux from one of the reservations near here. Dale said he would take me up there tomorrow to meet an old Indian shaman named Sam Going Away. He is the same man mentioned in the article I told you about."

"Yes, I remember," Holly said. "It was about the disputes over jurisdiction on Indian lands, wasn't it?"

David answered, "Yes, the article told about a man who had wandered onto the Indian reservation while being pursued by the police. He was taken in by Sam Going Away who refused to turn the man over to the state police. There wasn't much in the article, but I'd like to follow it up while I'm here."

"Who is Dale Spirit Wolf, then, and how does he fit into this?" Holly asked.

"He is a man I met last night at the bar down the street," David replied.

Holly said, "You went up there to go the bars, eh?"

David laughed without saying anything.

Holly asked, "He knows Sam Going Away?"

"It was luck, I guess. He knows him and promised to take me up to meet him tomorrow." David's excitement about the coming day showed in his voice and the increased speed of his words.

"You'll enjoy the trip I'm sure. I'm glad you are having fun with your work," Holly said.

David thought of the irony of her remark. Fun wasn't exactly the way he would have described the last few days. "I think it will be a better day than today." That, of course, was the truth. Most anything would be better than today.

Not even Holly's call lightened his mood. He was depressed.

The late news blared from the television describing the tragic accidental death of a tourist at Mount Rushmore. David learned nothing new from the broadcast, not even the name of the victim.

He clicked the remote, turned out the light, and pulled the covers over his shoulders, but he found no refuge in sleep.

The wind had come up, brewing a thunderstorm. Something brushed against the window, a branch, he thought. But there was no tree by his window. He pulled up the blanket and looked toward the window. Lightning flashed, and for a brief moment, he saw Seegook's "Seagod" standing between him and the window, shimmering in the light.

Chapter 10

The morning arrived about the same time David finally went to sleep. The hotel's wake-up call shot through his dreams and dragged him into the new day. Troubled by the images and events of the past few hours, David lay staring at the ceiling trying to make sense of it all. The image of "Seagod" standing before the lightning-lit window seared into his memory, he tried to imagine it was all a dream of his own making.

He struggled through the usually normal activities necessary to prepare for the day — a cup of coffee delivered to his door, a shave and shower. He sat in the chair, listless and mystified by it all. The shrill ringing of the phone startled him back to the present.

"Hey, bro!" The voice on the phone cheered David. He was glad for the distraction today. At least he wouldn't be alone with his thoughts. "A man alone is in bad company," he paraphrased some great wit.

"I'm in the lobby. Let's get going." Dale said with excitement generated by anticipation of their road trip.

David followed Dale out to a dilapidated junker of a pickup.

"We're going in this?" David asked in feigned disbelief. "You're even braver than I thought."

"Yeah, that's what I am. A real Indian Brave." Dale quipped back.

"Just out of curiosity, Dale. Can you get insurance on something like this — especially for the passenger's health?" David asked with a chuckle.

"You betcha. It's insured by the Indian Insurance Company. It's a real Indian car. You ever see one of them break down? They aren't any good until they have at least 200,000 miles and at least six wrecks. That's when you know you really got good wheels."

David climbed in and the pickup choked and smoked into a semblance of life. Dale laughed as it bounced forward and stopped several times, throwing David against the door. Soon, it was chugging down the road and they were on their way to meet Sam Going Away.

The town was soon left behind them, and the country unfolded in its morning splendor.

"It's going to take a while. It's about forty miles from here," Dale declared. "You're gonna see some of the most beautiful and wild scenery in the world. Better enjoy it. Not many of you white guys get to come out this way, you know."

Dale started to laugh and added, "The last ones were with Custer."

"Wrong, you just put him in the wrong battlefield. I know at least THAT much about history," David shot back.

"Well aren't you just so smart — is it historical or hysterical?" Dale laughed at his little joke.

They left the paved highway, and turned onto a narrow gravel road. David began to wonder if Dale's old pickup was capable of getting them there in one piece.

"How long have you had this pickup?" he asked Dale. The doubt in his voice was obvious.

"It was my uncle's. He gave it to me five years ago. I don't know how long he had it. It's a '68, and still has a good engine." Dale said.

They bumped along the road for a few moments before Dale added, "It's got a good driver, too, so don't be scared. The only thing it doesn't have is Allstate, but you're in good hands anyway."

Dale glanced over at David and flashed a bright smile. "You don't want any fancy car on these roads," he explained. "You want something that'll get you where you want to go. It's a long way between gas stations out here. You want reliability, not looks."

David was not convinced this junk heap was as reliable as Dale promised, but he had no choice but to trust Dale's judgment. It was too late to back out of the journey now. If nothing else, the trip could be an "adventure in travel." It was like riding a bucking bronco.

David hung on and gazed out the window. The clouds danced above the tops of the jagged, bare outcroppings of rock jutting up from the flat brown and green plains. He was hypnotized by the movement of the roadside as it sped past next to them.

The sun cast dark shadows in the deep crevices of the tortured landscape toward the horizon. David thought about the beauty and violence mixed, giving the land its character. The hills were so rugged and barren, and yet stunning in their magnificence.

David's imagination made him see warriors mounted on horses at the tops of the ridges. He thought he could make out the forms of buffalo grazing on the tender green shoots of the plains over which he and Dale journeyed. Were they real, or were they memories imprinted on the land, rising with the mists to show him a living history?

David felt honored to see such a place as this.

"What are you thinking about. You're kinda quiet," Dale shouted over the roar of the engine.

David glanced over to Dale who was leaning slightly forward with both hands on the steering wheel, struggling to control the machine in his grip. The window was open, and the ends of the red bandanna tied around Dale's head fluttered in the wind sweeping through it. David wondered how anyone could be heard above the din anyway. What else could he be but quiet in all this noise.

"I'm fascinated by this scenery," he yelled above the noise of the engine and wind.

"It's our sacred land, you know," Dale responded. "My ancestors hunted here. They followed the buffalo across the plains. They always returned to our sacred sites."

David asked, "Are you talking about the Black Hills, or the Badlands?"

He looked across the landscape. The interplay of sun and shadow painted images on the sculpted hills beyond.

"Both," Dale answered. "All the sacred land around here is important to us."

The pickup lurched and roared as it dodged rocks and ruts in what was supposed to be a road. The graveled road had run out a few miles back, and what lay before them was nothing more than a trail.

"Your great-grandfathers came here without treating this land as sacred," Dale continued. "They thought it wasn't worth anything so decided the Sioux could keep it. When someone found gold up here, your ancestors changed their minds."

Dale motioned toward the hills rising above the horizon, and resumed his story.

"The settlers decided their treaties didn't mean what they agreed to after all. The treaties said the land was ours as long as the grass is green and the water flows. I guess they decided the grass isn't green in the summer up here so the land wasn't ours anymore."

David said he knew many of the treaties had been broken when the terms were no longer convenient.

"All of them were broken," Dale yelled over the noisy engine. "The history of our relationship with the Federal government isn't called 'The Trail of Broken Treaties' for nothin'."

"I thought the Congress had some kind of special trust relationship with Indians," David said.

"Trust?" Dale exploded. He broke into laughter, aware of the irony of the history of federal-Indian relationships and how little trust remained between them. "It's called trust, all right, but how can you believe somebody who speaks with a 'forked tongue?' Like I said last night. We're stuck in this little communist experiment in the middle of a big, uncaring, uneducated democracy."

David watched Dale's face as he recounted the long list of grievances. Dale was intense, concentrating as much on his narrative as his driving.

"They tried to push us into any place they thought was worthless. It's been a constant battle for us. First it was gold and the miners, then the railroad. After the railroad came the farmers. The military was there for all the others. They are still here, running their tests on our land. They don't care what happens to it or to us."

David knew about the historical infringements on Indian land, but he did not understand what Dale was talking about with the military tests today. Dale continued his monologue before David could ask him to clarify his last statement.

"Now there are the politicians and the tourists. They think us Indians are good for tourism. It's ok to keep a few of us around as long as we put on a good show. We give the tourists a good evening's entertainment dancing for them at the local museum or pow-wow, then they will leave us alone."

Dale had not looked at David through the course of his monologue. He paused now, and glanced at David to gauge the effect of his speech on the White Man.

David asked, "Don't the dances and museums help keep the culture alive?"

Dale laughed and shook his head in a show of disbelief before giving his answer.

"We're not wooden Indians outside the general store. We aren't artifacts either. Everyone has an agenda. These people say they are helping us keep our culture alive because of whatever it is they are doing for us."

Dale paused to collect his thoughts and continued, "There are the politicians. They used to think we were good for pushing their social programs. Back in the 60's and early 70's, we had all kinds of politicians coming out to study us."

David asked, "Wasn't it part of the War on Poverty?"

Dale answered, "I guess. We had Kennedys and Johnsons every other week, checking up on our health and social conditions. It sounded great, but nothin' ever changed. Only the politicians changed. Now, they think they've given us everything to 'help us help ourselves.' It was only a way for them to feel less guilty about what their ancestors did to ours."

They bumped along in silence for a few minutes before Dale asked David, "How did you get interested in us?"

"Anthropology classes," David answered.

Dale looked over at David and smiled before launching into another area of grievances.

"I forgot the anthropologists and archaeologists."

"What do you mean?" David was puzzled.

"Archaeologists want to dig everything up in the name of science, including our ancestors and their graves. They put the bones of our fathers on display for tourists to gawk at. Our ancestors' skulls are studied for DNA and whatever else science can get out of them. They put our ancestors' clothes and grave goods in museums."

"Doesn't it help preserve them?" David asked.

"It doesn't say anything about our life and how things were used. Besides, grave goods are sacred objects. They belong to the dead. No one else has a right to them," Dale emphasized. "Only the dead have a right to them. How would you like it if we dug up your grandfather and studied his bones?"

David had not thought about how he would feel if a turn of events placed him in such a situation. He was beginning to understand Dale's line of reasoning, however, and how difficult it was for museums and scientists to reach ethical decisions about their collections.

Dale continued, "The museums display anything, even sacred pipes no one but the caretaker was supposed to see. Now anyone can see them. It's not right."

David watched Dale's face with fascination. He could see how deeply offended Dale felt by the centuries of oppression and well-intentioned patronization his people had suffered. Dale launched into a new grievance.

"The anthropologists want us to live in a museum," Dale gestured helplessly in frustration. "They don't want us to have radios and TVs. We aren't supposed to have contact with anybody but them. These social scientists say they are saving our culture for us."

Dale shifted gears as the pickup lurched over a gopher hole.

"According to them," he said, "it is damaging our culture if we have running water, electricity, flush toilets, and hospital care. Since our ancestors didn't have these things, we aren't supposed to either."

Dale paused, then continued.

"They measure our heads and count our teeth, and compare us to their other 'natural' species. They don't think of us as humans. We're just 'subjects' for their study. They get their Phd's, then try to get rich and famous describing how we live, but they don't want it to ever change. We aren't supposed to want the good things they have because it might make us less 'Indian'."

David interjected a question. It was the first chance he had to say anything.

"How can an Indian be 'less Indian'?"

Dale glanced over at him and smiled as though he understood the confusion. Dale explained, "I had an Eskimo friend once who told me he liked McDonald's better than seal liver these days. He asked me if he was still an Eskimo because he did not eat traditional foods anymore," Dale said as he glanced up at David. "I think he'd be an Eskimo no matter what he ate, because he *is* an Eskimo. Have you heard of Italian-Americans who don't like spaghetti?"

"Yes, I've known some before," David replied.

"Do you think they were still Italian-Americans?" Dale asked.

"They only spoke Italian when they could. I guess it makes them Italian." David said.

"We should be able to have individual tastes and choices in life just like Europeans," Dale's explosive voice rose over the roar of the engine. "No one else gets accused of losing their culture just because they don't eat traditional foods."

David was surprised, if not shocked by Dale's outburst.

"I never thought about it before in those terms. I always assumed people preferred the older ways and resisted change. My teachers always implied the anthropologists were protecting Native people from exploitation and cultural changes brought by missionaries."

"Don't get me started on missionaries," Dale said with less anger in his voice. "At least I have to admit many of them had good intentions. They just didn't understand the actual situation."

David gazed at the passing scenery, thinking about Dale's emotional outburst. He finally voiced his agreement. "It should be the people themselves who decide what kinds of changes should be made and when. You are right, people should not be 'preserved' in a 'living' museum. Nobody I know would want to go back to living without electricity and running water."

"You better believe it," Dale agreed. "No matter how much some of the Yuppies in the '70's talked about going back to the land, they weren't about to go back to raising their own crops or hunting and fishing. They couldn't live without all the gadgets they grew up with. Most of them never would have survived without Safeway."

David laughed as he imagined the sight of his friends from the beach trying to hunt for their food.

Dale said, "It is good my people never had a lot of those material things. Since they had to work for their food, it made them strong. It is easier for us to survive hardship, because we are already at a subsistence level. We know how to survive."

David thought he could sense a certain pride in Dale's voice. He also understood how much freedom there could be knowing there was nothing to lose.

"It doesn't mean we should be deprived of something better if we want it," Dale said. "Non-Indians who don't understand anything about our lives, culture, or religion have no right to tell us what material things we should give up."

They bounced along the narrow, rocky path. Dale started to laugh to himself. David looked over toward him, puzzlement on his face.

"What's so funny?" David asked.

"I was just thinking about how we are stereotyped by everybody," Dale answered.

"I don't understand what you are talking about. What do you mean?" David asked Dale to clarify his comment.

"Have you ever heard of the Atlanta Rednecks?" Dale asked in a serious tone, followed by a burst of laughter.

It took a minute for David to get the point of the joke. He joined in with his own contribution.

"I see. Have you heard of the Washington Whiteskins?"

Dale came back with another, "How about the Cleveland Jews?"

The point had been made. David had not thought much about the way Indians are used as mascots for sports teams, along with rams, bulls, and birds. The tension David had felt when Dale was talking about anthropologists and museums had dissipated with their banter over the mascot names.

David fell into silence, watching the landscape unfold mile by mile. The pickup's engine roared and groaned as it struggled over the rocks and holes in what was still called a road. It was Dale's turn to express curiosity.

"You mentioned the other night you were here on an assignment. Why would the LA Sun Times be sending a reporter all the way out to South Dakota?"

David studied Dale's profile and considered how much he should tell Dale.

"Did you known anything about a Hollywood studio set up here?" He paused a moment, collecting his thoughts. "I'm supposed to find out if it has anything to do with weapons testing. My boss thought something was odd about the whole thing. He wanted me to find out what kind of story, if any, there was in it."

Dale masked any surprise he might have felt, "Isn't it a long shot to send somebody all the way out from California?"

"I don't think so. The paper sends people out on wild goose chases all the time. How do you think we get our stories? Wait for a tip? The news profession has people everywhere, and they send more when a story breaks."

"Maybe your paper received a tip on this one. Was it an informer you met yesterday?" Dale asked, his curiosity grown more evident in his voice.

David stared at Dale. He did not know how much he should say, and chose caution.

"There was a mix-up in communication. We never met."

"Were you supposed to meet him at Mount Rushmore?" Dale asked. David watched for any betrayal of emotion on Dale's face. He wondered what Dale knew and how Dale could have guessed his arrangements.

"Do you know what happened at Mount Rushmore?" David asked, stunned.

"Maybe the mix-up was because he died before he could talk," Dale answered, looking straight ahead at the road.

"What are you saying?" David demanded.

"I know about the guy who went off the cliff up there. He didn't fall. One of our people was there and saw someone push him." Dale turned and looked at David with a burning intensity.

David felt sick. Now he was sure the dead man had been his contact. He did not know how Dale could be involved in any of this. There was nothing to lose by asking Dale to disclose all he knew.

"I suspected he had been. I was not sure until now he was the man I was supposed to meet," David admitted. "What do you know about it?"

"Not much," Dale said. "I know there are lots of government secrets people in power wouldn't want you to uncover. They wouldn't want any reporters out snooping around with disgruntled employees."

"You think this guy had something to tell me, then?" David asked.

"He contacted you, didn't he? I don't know who he was," Dale said. "I only know some of my friends have been monitoring illegal government activities near the reservation."

David asked, "How did they get involved?"

"The questionable activities are taking place on land we think is ours. The military took it over. Since then, some weird things have been going on," Dale answered.

"Like what?" David probed.

"They are doing tests we think might harm the environment. We think they might be using Indians as guinea pigs for their experiments." Dale glanced at David whose every sense was alert.

"We've been following them for a couple of years," continued Dale. "We hoped we could expose what they are doing, and also get the land back."

"What does this have to do with the dead man?" asked David.

Dale answered, "Some of those people from the facility were up at the Park yesterday. One of them pushed the 'tourist' over the cliff. We didn't know why. If you came up here on a tip, it would make more sense, wouldn't it?"

"I suppose it would," David said. "The man calls me and they find out."

Dale picked up the story. "They kill him before he can tell you whatever it was he wanted you to know. The catch is they don't know we saw them do it."

"They wouldn't know we would run into each other in some bar, or about my interest in meeting some old Indian man you knew," David continued. "You know, I received a couple of messages warning me about meeting this guy."

"When?" Dale asked.

"The first one was at the airport when I arrived. Then they called my hotel," David explained. "They seemed to know who I was and why I was there."

"Whoever they are, they are still following you," Dale said, his voice dry and rasping.

"Following me?" Dale said, surprised. "What do you mean?"

"See the helicopter over to the right?" Dale pointed as he spoke.

David strained to make out the profile of a helicopter low above the jagged horizon. It seemed far away. He could not see how this made Dale's remark any more clear.

"It's been following us for the past hour," Dale explained. "It circles back for a while then goes to the left. I think they are trying to look like a training flight, but they are always the same distance from us."

David's heart started to pound.

Dale returned to his narrative. "I can tell you something else about the tests. They lost one of their experiments out here. I think it was some kind of a rocket or satellite or something, but it crashed. We think it belonged to these people. Some of our plants saw it come down and got out there soon after the crash. They wanted to salvage what they could before anyone else made it out there," Dale paused, looking towards David. "You want to see the site?"

David could not believe his good fortune. "Of course! When can you take me?"

"It's close to here. We'll talk about it after we see Sam," Dale promised.

They had driven to the end of a road and arrived at the top of a plateau overlooking a canyon. A short distance from the cliff stood a ramshackle hut of wood and tin. Several old cars rusted in the grassland surrounding the shack and old oil drums littered the ground.

Some fifty feet away was a dome-shaped structure, which Dale explained was Sam's sweathouse.

"Sam will probably invite you to the sweathouse. You should go," Dale instructed David.

The pickup ground to a halt. Two dogs ran to the vehicle, jumping at the door while howling their greeting to the two men. David and Dale left the pickup and stumbled over the dogs on the path to the shack.

"Do you have something to give to Sam?" Dale asked.

David did not know such protocol was required. "What should I have brought?" he asked, already concerned he had done something wrong.

"You could give him your watch," Dale answered and smiled at him with a good-natured jest. "You give him what he thinks is nice."

"How will I know what it should be?" David was still confused. He did not know if Dale was serious or not.

"In our way, if you say you like something, then it means you'd like to have it. If he compliments you on something, then give it to him," Dale explained the procedure.

"What are you giving him?" David inquired.

"You're the one coming to see him," Dale answered. "I'm just your guide." Dale reached the door before he added, "I've brought cigarettes for him."

David felt uneasy. He was glad to have this experience, but he sometimes felt lost and alone. "Well, it's too late to back out now," David thought to himself. "I'm just going to have to enjoy meeting an Indian shaman." The door to the shack opened.

Chapter 11

The old man who appeared at the doorway was a tall but slightly stooped Indian wearing a tattered and sweat-lined cowboy hat, blue jeans, plaid shirt, and well-worn cowboy boots. His face looked like the land from which he came: deep crevices scarred the smooth surface of his face like canyon walls, and his black eyes were like the reflective pools of water which gathered in the lowlying ponds.

His skin was the color of the painted desert at sunset when the sand and sun combined to cast a reddish hue over the brown landscape. Like the Badlands, the wind and weather had sculpted his features. His wispy white hair was pulled back from the balding forehead and gathered at the nape of his neck. Stray strands blew in the breeze like tumbleweeds running across the countryside.

The old man wobbled a bit on his rubbery legs, but still carried himself with great dignity and authority. He extended his great, immense hand to Dale, then to David.

David noticed how long his arms were, and how his hand, though large and strong, had a kind gentleness in the firm grip. These hands had surely served the old man well through the years, David mused. Like his face, the skin was smooth, but leathery, made hard by the decades of exposure to natural elements and physical hardship. They were not the hands of a lazy man.

David's thoughts continued to flow as his imagination was fired by the earthiness of this old man. It seemed the old man might disappear into the ground if he were to lay down on it. He was so similar to the land itself, he was part of it. David could understand now how stories like the "Sleeping Ute" could become legendary.

He had forgotten the mountain with the name "Sleeping Ute" for years. When he was a kid, he had visited relatives in Cortez,

Colorado and had been told about the legend of the mountain with the shape of an Indian's head and body. This, said the story, was the sleeping form of a great Ute chief who would someday rise from his slumbers to lead his people to freedom. Like the "Sleeping Ute," Sam Going Away seemed one with the environment that gave him life.

David became aware of the old man's voice, speaking to him in words he could not understand. He assumed Dale and Sam were speaking in the Oglala Lakota dialect.

Dale turned to face David before addressing him with the translation of Sam's words.

"He says, 'Welcome to the home he shares with Mother Earth.' He wants us to come in and have some frybread and coffee."

David was nervous and uncertain. "What should I do? Do I give him a gift now, or what?"

Dale responded with obvious amusement at David's discomfort. "After we visit for a while, then offer him your gift out of respect for his hospitality."

The dogs continued to jump around the three men in excited anticipation and ran to and fro as the group stood at the door of the hut. David was aware of the chirps of birds voicing their welcome, too. He felt a warm sense of strange familiarity which gradually was replacing his nervous uncertainty. He stepped across the threshold into the dwelling.

It took a few moments for David's eyes to adjust to the relative darkness of the simple, one-room cabin. After they became accustomed to the variation of light from the bright sunshine outside, David began to examine the surroundings in the plain but tidy hut.

Everything, like the old man himself, belonged to the earth. There was apparently no electricity, as oil lamps hung from the ceiling and illuminated the table in the middle of the room. To one side, a wooden frame held the single bed covered in wool blankets. At the other end was a stone oven of sorts, a kind of fireplace and oven combined, constructed with wires and an iron sheet on the top for cooking. It looked like the kind of contraption the old man would have built himself. The entire hut and its contents was probably his own handiwork.

The walls and floor were of wood, decorated with the necessities of life for a man living on his own. There were snowshoes, rifles, coats, buckets, and many sheaves of dried flowers and herbs along the walls and rafters. The latter, David thought, must have been grown or gathered by Sam, dried and stored here for future use.

Sam observed David looking at the dried shrubs and commented about them. Dale translated the speech, but the words did not make sense to David. Dale said, "There are more plants in this world than those given by Mother Earth." David nodded, although he was in complete confusion. He decided to ask Dale what it meant later.

Dale and David were invited to sit at the table. It, too, was of rough hewn wood. Sam brought over a coffee pot from the "stove" in one hand and three tin cups in his other. David recognized the coffee pot as one like he used to use when he went camping. It brought back memories.

They were seated on homemade chairs, drinking coffee from tin cups, and eating frybread offered to them from a hand thrown and fired pottery plate. David thought it seemed such a simple and yet productive life in its way.

David glanced out one of the four windows. There was one on each wall of the cabin. The scenery was beautiful. It was wild and barren, yet spectacular with the ever-changing shadows and colors painted by the sun.

This seemed so far from his own life in the city. He felt in a different world and a different time. He could almost hear the quiet.

The crackle of the twentieth century came in the guise of a battery-powered CB radio.

"This radio, Sam's neighbors insisted he have it. They were worried about how isolated he is out here," Dale explained. "Sam didn't want it much. Doesn't bother him any being out here alone. He's close to the land and he knows how to live with nature. But some of his neighbors have lost that gift. They think you need technology to survive."

"So why did Sam say ok to such an intrusive presence?" David asked.

"He didn't want to be 'troublesome,' Dale explained. "He knows his neighbors have good hearts and want to take care of him. They just don't really understand that he doesn't need it like they do."

Dale was summoned to speak to the caller on the crackling box. David continued to sip coffee and eat his frybread as Dale visited with the disembodied voice. When he returned to the table, Dale provided a rough translation of the conversation for David's benefit.

"The caller was a friend of mine who lives down the road. He checks up on Sam. He said he saw us driving down here. He just called to say hi and find out how long we are going to be here."

David expressed surprise they had been noticed. "I didn't see anyone on the way here. Where did he see us?"

Dale smiled and contemplated the coffee tin in his hands before telling David, "You might think you are out here in the middle of nowhere, but there are plenty of eyes scanning the horizons. We have always been known for our sharpened senses," he pointed to his eyes. "Our lives depended on knowing what is happening on the hills and prairies. We've not forgotten how to watch and listen. There aren't many secrets kept for long, even around here."

The three men continued to drink coffee and eat fry-bread in silence. The quiet seemed awkward to David. He felt as if someone should be saying something. His two companions seemed quite natural and at ease. They were comfortable with the silence only occasionally interrupted by the sounds of barking dogs. David absent-mindedly pulled out his keys and rubbed the little ivory carving which hung from the ring. He often did this out of habit when he was thinking or was nervous. Like a worry bead, he had been told once, that old Greek men rub when they sit outside the doors of their shops.

It seemed an eternity they had been sitting with their coffees in the silence. Sam spoke to David with a slight gesture of his hand. David could not understand what Sam said and looked to Dale for guidance.

"He says you have a nice carving," Dale said. David took the hint and handed it across the table to Sam with a silent smile, but not one he felt inside. This was not something he wanted to part with.

David was sentimental. This was one of the few things he had carried with him from his days in Alaska. He had watched Old Man Koongoosuk carve the little figure. It was a billikin, a gift from the old man to him when he was young.

"You keep this with you, little Gussuk" the old man had told him.

"What is it, grandpa?" David had asked him. It was such a strange little figure and not very pretty.

"It's billikin. He brings you good luck. You rub his belly," Koongoosuk told him.

David looked at the little figure as it left his hands as he passed it across the table to Sam. It had a pointed head and large eyes that slanted upward. It's crooked, crazy smile gaped like some toothless grandfather. It had a round, fat stomach, rubbed smooth from the many years it had been polished under David's thumb.

He hated the thought of losing his good-luck charm, but more than that, he hated to part with something of Koongoosuk he felt he had that was tangible when he held the little figure. But then he almost heard Old Man Koongoosuk's voice in his ear.

"You keep this. But you don't own it. It is a gift to you to keep and take care of. Someday, you give it somebody important and it will bring you more luck than if you try to hang onto it." Maybe this was the time he was supposed to let go of it and send it into someone else's care.

"My Eskimo grandfather gave it to me, and I give it to you," David said softly. David meant it, and was pleased to see Sam beam broadly when Dale translated the words to him.

Sam's weathered hand received the gift. He looked carefully at the carving. Sam rose from the table and returned with a blank sheet of paper. Sam sat down and drew a quick sketch on the paper.

David was amazed at the Sam's artistic talent. But he was stunned when Sam passed it across the table to him. Before him was the face of Old Man Koongoosuk. He felt faint.

"This is Old Man Koongoosuk," David said in disbelief. "How did you know him?"

Sam was smiling at him. He said something to Dale.

"He saw him when he looked at the carving just now," Dale said.

"But that's impossible. He's been dead for years." David could not understand how Sam could see into the past just by looking at something.

"I told you he is not like other men," Dale said. "I told you he can fly. They probably met each other on some other world."

David felt like he was dreaming.

"He wants to know if you like it?"

"It's remarkable." David said, still stunned by the revelation of some unknown force that could render time and space meaningless and before his very eyes.

"He learned to draw from looking at nature. Remember what I said about our sense of observation, that is how he learned," Dale said.

David said, "I feel like he has looked right through me and into my past."

"Maybe he has," Dale said. "He can look into your eyes and read your soul. I think he likes what he has read. Do you like the drawing?"

David smiled, then said, "Of course I do."

"He wants you to have it," Dale said.

David knew that anything he lost by giving away the billikin was more than replaced by Koongoosuk's portrait, drawn by a man who had never set eyes on him — at least as far as David knew.

"This is his gift to you," Dale explained. "He doesn't have much, as you can see. In our way, even the most humble person can offer something to another."

David could feel his heart beating as he looked first into Sam's deep eyes and then at the sketch in his hand. He was grateful for the experience and the tangible reminder of it.

The exchange made the carving he had received years before take on a new and different meaning and memory, of which he would be reminded by the drawing. This is what was meant by riches returning to the giver, a concept this culture had never forgotten. This is just what Old Man Koongoosuk had told him years earlier.

David had to remind himself of his purpose in meeting Sam. The wonder of the new experiences and generosity of his companions was enough to make him nearly forget why he had come here.

"Sam has been so generous and kind to me. I know he was kind to another stranger, too. Would you ask him to tell me about the man he took care of and where he is now?" David asked Dale to convey his thanks and the request to Sam.

Dale spoke to Sam, who said a few words while looking at David. Dale turned to David and translated Sam's comment, "Sam says you will meet this man when the time is right. You are not ready yet."

David asked Dale, "Do you know what he means, or when I'll be ready?"

"I don't. But he says you will meet his guest the next time you come here." Dale seemed as mystified by Sam's answer as David was.

"I did not know I would be back here," David admitted to Dale.

"He says you will return after a trip. Are you planning another trip?" Dale asked David.

"I am going to Gallup after I leave here. It has to do with the meeting we talked about on the way up here. Does he mean I am supposed to come back here before I go home, or come here later?" David asked for clarification of Sam's comments. He was beginning to believe the old man had not only seen David's past when he drew the portrait, but also into his future.

Dale spoke to Sam, who gave his reply. Dale wrote something on another piece of paper provided by Sam. Dale gave it to David with Sam's instructions.

"When you go to Gallup, you are to go and see a Navajo friend of Sam's. He has something to send to Sam, and you could bring it back for him. These are the numbers and instructions you will need to contact him and find your way to his hogan. Sam will send word to him to tell him you are coming there."

David took the paper and agreed to get in touch with Sam's friend while he was in the Southwest. He had the feeling this whole journey had already been planned for him.

Sam arose from the table and began to prepare a lunch for his guests. David watched Sam as he stood at the stove. He sensed Sam Going Away was about to satisfy something more than the physical hunger inside him.

Chapter 12

After lunch, Sam took Dale and David to a special place near his hut. David learned through Dale about the rings of stones on the ground before them. These were "teepee rings," or stones once used to hold down the edges of the teepees of many generations of ancestors who had once camped here.

Dale explained to David in a dramatic narrative, "Our grandfathers moved from place to place following the buffalo, which they hunted for food, clothing, and shelter. These rings are found at many sites along the migration trail," he said as he pointed to the rings of stones. "They would go from one of these sites to another. The rings showed where the encampment would be. These places have special historical and spiritual meaning to our people today."

David felt closer to the land than ever before. He absorbed the sun and air like a sponge, drawing strength from the sacred earth around him. He had rarely felt so refreshed. Then something strange happened. The sun began to shimmer and take on a different shape. Legs seemed to drop down from the bright disk of the sun, and once again, David saw the shining image of "Seagod" before him. Like some reluctant Scrooge, he felt compelled to follow the specter before him. He was somehow transported to a different time or place.

"But it is the same place," David thought in confusion. Teepee rings were still in place, but instead of Sam and Dale, David saw ghosts rising along the horizon like heat waves. He felt sorrow and pain, like his inner soul was being torn out of his body. Their fearful aspect became ever more real as bloodied corpses of the long dead victims of a new technology staggered past him unaware of his power to see them.

As soon as it had come upon him, the vision was replaced by the mundane, and he was back in the twentieth century.

David realized Dale was staring at him in concern. Sam, on the other hand, was some distance away, selecting plants for medicines.

"Hey, you look pale, even for a pale-face," Dale tried to joke with him. "You ok?"

"I don't know what happened. I think I had a vision or something," David admitted almost to himself.

"You were just staring into the distance. You didn't answer when I talked to you," Dale said.

"I couldn't hear you. All I could see were bodies around here. You and Sam weren't here anymore," David answered.

"Yeah, you had a vision all right. There was a massacre here back in about 1888. I think our people showed themselves to you," Dale was a little pale himself.

Sam came back to the quiet and confused pair of men, but seemed undisturbed by their changed mood. Instead, he spoke to Dale.

"He knows all about your vision," Dale explained. "He says you will suffer before you are taught the way you are to go. You have been chosen, though, to help us."

"Help you how?" David asked in disbelief.

"You will know, Sam says. But he says we must go now." Dale said as he began to follow Sam.

David was almost angry. He wanted answers now. What had happened to him? What was happening to him now? Why did it seem everyone in the world knew everything about him and what he was to do except him? He dragged along behind, knowing he was not going to have his questions answered right now.

The men returned reluctantly to Sam's hut as the sun was casting long fingers of shadows across the landscape. The clouds floating like great ships had sails painted red and gold. The sky deepened into a dark purple before the first stars began to light the night.

Sam prepared a simple supper of bread, cold meat, and tea. When the meal was finished, David was invited to join his two companions in Sam's sweat lodge. This, Dale explained, was a ritual of spiritual cleansing for David.

Sam disappeared into the night to prepare the lodge. Dale explained to David how Sam would heat the lodge so it would provide steam like a sauna.

Dale and David left the warm light of Sam's hut to make the short journey down the path to the sweat lodge. David was struck by the stillness of the night. Stars were shining now, but the moon had not yet risen. All was quiet. Nothing but the breeze in the willows broke the heavy silence of the blanketing darkness.

The sweat lodge was a dugout covered with sod and skins. The entrance was almost underground and David had to bend down to his knees to enter.

"You go in naked and backwards," Dale explained to him. "It's like you are returning into the womb of the Mother Earth that gave you life."

It was fitting, he thought, to have to enter such a place with humility. It had been a long time since he had felt so humble. After today, he felt like a newborn babe — without understanding, in need of care.

Inside, the hut was pitch black except for the glowing of the rocks in the fire. There was a hissing sound as Dale poured water on the hot rocks. The steam made curious shapes, like ghosts of warriors from the past, as it rose and glowed above the red heat.

Sam was seated cross-legged on the ground at the opposite end. He chanted in a low voice, and the music rose with the steam, floated from the lodge upward to the stars above.

David felt the oppressive heat, and became lightheaded. The music of Sam's chanting, the glowing apparitions above the fire, and the wet heat of the steam, combined to free his spirit from his body.

David sensed he was floating near the roof of the lodge. If he had wished, he thought he could have floated up through the smokehole and into the night. It was only when he felt a pair of hands moving along his sweaty back and shoulders he returned to his physical body. The hands came to rest on his head.

These massive hands could only belong to Sam Going Away. David again lost track of his own consciousness. He was vaguely aware of the chants which continued to fill the cramped surroundings of the steaming enclosure. It seemed to spin around him. He no longer knew anything. Who he was, why he was here. Only that something outside his understanding and control, some greater force, was driving him into unexpected and uncharted journeys.

Some time later, he was not sure how long, he realized he was cold. He was standing beside Dale beneath the night sky.

The moon cast its blue shadows on the path as the breeze rustled the bushes beside it. Somewhere, far away in the distance, David heard the ghostly yelp of a coyote, which soon rose into a chorus of howls from the pack. He shivered with awe, at once moved by the eerieness of the music and overwhelmed by its beauty.

"They are welcoming you," Dale said to him.

They stood and listened in the chill until the coyotes' chorus subsided, then continued in silence up the path. A different call broke the stillness.

"Whoo-whoo, whoo-whoo." David heard the owl's call.

It swooped down from the blackness above, flashes of moonlight reflected on its feathery wings. David was in awe, but sensed an immediate change in the mood of his companions.

Dale glanced apprehensively at the solemn Sam, who watched the bird as it landed on the bush before them. The owl stared at Sam with its large round eyes that looked like two pools of water, then swiftly rose again to disappear into the light of the moon.

No one said anything, and David could not understand the change in the atmosphere. It was only later, when Sam walked them to the pickup, that David began to understand what the message of the owl had been.

"The owl brings news of death," Sam said quietly, in English.

Dale asked, "Who is he calling?"

"He's calling David's name" Sam replied.

David did not know what Sam meant. He felt disconnected anyway, as if he didn't care.

Dale glanced at him for a moment before he spoke. "Sam wanted you to hear about the owl's message. It is a warning for you. It's bad to see an owl on a night like this," Dale added. David noticed the fear in Dale's voice. Something had scared him.

"Why?" David asked.

"Death is part of life, too. We have to remember that." Dale said.

David thought in silence for a moment before he spoke. "If we are to accept death as part of life, then it should not be a bad thing to see the owl, should it?"

"You are right," Dale answered, lapsing into a philosophical monologue. "We forget how we are to see the world, and how we are to live in it. Death is merely another step in our lives, but we try to resist because we are holding on to other parts of living."

While Dale seemed scared by the owl, Sam was matter-of-fact. David could tell that they each understood something different about what had happened. For Sam, it just seemed part of what David was going to have to endure. David, for his own part, felt exhausted and could no longer make sense of any of it.

David watched the moon-saturated hills march past the black sky with its pinholes of light. The bushes along the road raced past in a blur as they came into the brilliance of the headlights, then ran to hide again in the shadows.

The screech of the owl filled David's ears, and its glowing eyes pierced through him no matter which way he turned. The owl's warning of impending death sent a shiver through his bones.

Chapter 13

The pickup bounced along the road for a few miles, then turned onto a narrow dirt path. The pickup's headlights lit up the house which came into view. Dogs ran up to the pickup, as they had to Sam Going Away's hut. They barked and jumped at the doors of the pickup, announcing the arrival of guests. Dale read David's thoughts and answered his unspoken question.

"This is where we'll stay tonight," Dale stated as they pulled to a stop beyond the gate. "It belongs to the friend I talked with up at Sam's so he is expecting us. He will go with us tomorrow to where that rocket or whatever it was crashed."

David was not convinced their arrival was expected, but the way he felt right then, he didn't care. The long-haired man silhouetted against the light pouring through the open door carried a rifle in his arms.

His doubts were soon dispelled. The gun dropped to the man's side. He bounded up to the vehicle with as much energy as his dogs had shown a few minutes earlier.

"Hey, Lester," Dale slapped Lester on the back in a good-natured greeting after he stepped out of the pickup.

"Hi-yah, Dale," the owner of the house responded. "Is this your white man friend?"

"Meet David. He belongs to some tribe or other judging by his name, Seabird," Dale joked as he introduced David.

"Seabird, eh?" the man repeated. "Your name's more Indian than mine!"

David enjoyed the banter between the two friends and returned the greeting with an extended hand. The cloud hanging over him began to dissipate and his own mood lightened as he was distracted from his dark thoughts.

"David, this is Lester Hair-Hangs-Loose," Dale continued the introductions. Lester grasped David's hand with a firm grip and shook with the enthusiasm of a man who likes meeting other people.

David smiled, then observed, "It sounds to me like your name is more Indian than mine!"

Lester laughed then said, "Mine doesn't have any helpers in it."

David did not understand what Lester meant by the statement. "What are you saying? What are the helpers in my name?" he asked.

"Spirit helpers," Lester replied. "You have a seabird helper. They take the forms of birds, animals, fish, sea mammals. It's good to have a spirit helper with you, so you have a good name."

They entered Lester's house before Dale asked him about the rifle Lester still held in his hand. Lester's voice was calm and soft as he explained, "I knew you were coming, but I wasn't sure when. I had to be certain it was you."

Dale and David exchanged puzzled glances. Dale asked, "Who else are you expecting?"

"I don't know if I'm expecting anyone else or not. There are some strange things happening around here. It started with the business on the hill." Lester pulled a chair away from the table and sat down. He motioned for them to join him. David had no idea what "that business" might be, but realized Dale understood Lester's meaning.

Lester continued, "We've seen government cars, helicopters, those kinds of things. I'm sure we're being watched. It's best to be careful. I'm not surrendering without a fight."

The matter of fact tone with which Lester made this promise sent a chill down the back of David's neck. He said nothing, but could sense the electric energy of intrigue.

He was uneasy, recalling the face of the man who had been retrieved from the bottom of the cliff at Mount Rushmore. He saw the burning eyes of the owl which had glowed at him earlier in the evening. David was aware of the eerie connection of the two events which before seemed worlds apart.

Lester got up from the table, went to the refrigerator, and returned with three bottles. Lester offered his guests the beer. David looked around at the house.

The fact there was little furniture gave the rooms in view a cavernous feel. They needed something to soak up all the extra space, David thought. The chair and couch with their wooden frames and red and blue cushions looked like government issues David had seen in military homes.

The well-worn kitchen table had a yellow Formica top with chrome legs and trim. It reminded David of the photographs he had seen of lower middle class houses in the 1950's and 1960's when everyone was pleased to have the latest in mass-produced modern furniture. The chairs did not match the table, but seemed to belong to a different set of the same variety and period of functional kitchen furnishings.

The cupboards lining the walls of the kitchen were constructed of white-painted plywood. The fluorescent light tubes in the ceiling gave the room a cold, bluish tint.

In the corner of the living room there was a large bookcase. David could see Lester was an avid reader. To his surprise, there was also a computer desk, office chair and several filing cabinets. The corner made a well-equipped office.

David had not expected such a fine office from his first impression of the house. Lester noticed the interest in David's eyes, and volunteered an explanation.

"You see here my BIA castle and corporate suite. This side is my castle," he said as he gestured toward the kitchen and part of the living room, "and there is my executive office."

"What do you do for a living?" David asked.

"I'm a high paid independent Indian consultant," Lester said with amusement echoed by Dale's own laughter.

"He's one of those rip-off artists, in other words," Dale chimed in as he raised his bottle to Lester in a salute.

"Ha! I earned the right to the title, and to every cent I make!" Lester shot back, smiling.

"You still didn't answer my question," David observed, trying to fit the image of this tall Indian in a headband and long black hair with one of a corporate executive.

Lester was not dressed like any consultant David was likely to see in the city. David tried to imagine what Lester would look like in a three-piece suit. His blue jeans, leather vest, and red flannel shirt looked so much more natural. Lester had an elaborate beaded belt buckle at his waist. David could not imagine how it would look with a three-piece suit.

"It's true I am a consultant," Lester said. "I didn't go to Harvard University for nothin' you know."

"Harvard?" David asked, not certain whether to believe him or not. "How did you happen to go there?"

"It's a long story," Lester began. "I went to elementary school here on the reservation. When we reached high school, we had to leave the reservation and were sent off to boarding school. Mine was in Kansas."

"Wasn't it hard to leave home when you were so young?" David asked, appalled to think of what it must have been like to be sent away from home to go to school.

"Sure, it was traumatic. It was hard for everyone, not just us kids. We didn't get to know our culture as well as we might have because we were isolated from it. Our grandparents never had the chance to know us as teenagers when they could have helped us with many of the transitions in our lives," Lester explained.

"How did your parents feel about it?" David inquired.

"What could they do? It was the way things were then. They would say sometimes it was good for us. Some said the BIA was only helping us to get a better education than we could in small villages and on reservations." Lester took a handful of peanuts from a dish in the center of the table and began to chew one thoughtfully.

"I was sent to Oklahoma for a few years," Dale said. "Sometimes, we thought it was exciting to be out on our own, but Lester is right. It was hard on everyone."

Lester continued his story. "When I was in school, I had this good teacher who took an interest in several of us. He wanted us to succeed and helped us understand the importance of education in a white man's world. I was a wild one before he came there. He helped me get my act together."

David had no difficulty seeing how Lester might have been a handful for most teachers. He still looked wild!

"The teacher helped me apply for the Indian program at Harvard. I got in," Lester said. "I was proud of my academic achievement because it is an important school and I worked hard to succeed there."

"Great help it's been since then, though," Lester said with bitterness.

"You come back and find out getting an education makes some of your neighbors think you've sold out to the white man. They don't think your an Indian anymore," Lester paused and sipped his beer. "The white man thinks you're an uppity Indian who got into an ivy league school just because of race. They only had the chance to go to some Podunk State University for their education, so they are jealous of you. You just can't win."

"I had no idea people would make it so difficult. I always heard how great Harvard was. The possibility a degree from there could be a liability never occurred to me," David said.

"When you can't win, you have to find some other way," Lester continued. "I came back to the reservation and set up my own business. I can work out of my home here, but don't have to rely on reservation politics. I can have the best of both worlds. I live where I want, work when I want, and have to answer only to myself."

David could see the advantages of the arrangement. He was almost jealous of Lester's freedom.

"My modem ties me to the rest of the world. I can sit here and write grants, help Indian colleges design curricula. Since I have a legal degree, too, I can consult Indian organizations about their legal needs. It's a good life," Lester concluded.

"It gives me time to help out on other issues, too. We're working on getting back the land taken by the military near here. I give a little advice to these young bucks like Dale, here, and do my best to keep them out of trouble."

Dale piped up with mock indignation, "I'm not such an idiot!"

Lester and Dale laughed at some inside joke. Lester admitted, "It's true. Did you know your friend Dale is another educated Indian?"

David looked over at Dale, who beamed with pride.

"Yeah, I'm not as uppity as this Harvard jock, but mine wasn't any 'Podunk U,' either — University of Minnesota, Civil Engineering degree," Dale said proudly. "I'm working for the tribe these days. But I'm like Lester. We're more interested right now in getting our land back and keeping the military off it."

David felt almost embarrassed. "You two guys have more education than I do. You seem so comfortable in your surroundings. Tell me why."

"It's our roots. We have a long culture to sustain us," Lester said. He continued, "Our peoples' territory included most of North and South Dakota, and parts of Nebraska and Wyoming. At the center of all of this was the sacred place, the Black Hills. They came here to pay homage to the Creator."

David watched Dale's reaction to Lester's explanation. He could see the pride written on Dale's face as Dale took up the narrative.

"It is a special place for our people as the center of all creation and the source of all life. This is where the spiritual leaders of all our nations gathered for special ceremonies. It is the most special of all our sacred sites."

Lester then continued, "It was so sacred no one could live there. Only those who were specially prepared could go into this sacred region."

David commented, "I remember reading how the Black Hills made up part of the most sacred lands taken by the white men because of the discovery of gold there. How did the Ft. Laramie treaty fit into all of this?"

Lester looked at David in surprise and said, "I'm surprised you know anything about the Ft. Laramie treaty at all! Most Americans have forgotten about it and the rest of the treaties, too."

Dale continued, "You must have heard about the 'Trail of Broken Treaties?'"

"Yes," David answered, "I think I read something saying all the treaties made with Indian peoples had been broken at one time or another."

"It's true," Lester continued. "Our people were rounded up over a hundred years ago and forced to live on land the white men thought had no value. By the 1860's, white hunters and settlers were killing off the buffalo. This was a great tragedy for our ancestors."

Dale elaborated on the thought. "The buffalo were an important source of food. Their hides were used for clothing and shelter. The buffalo were important for more than physical needs of our people, though. The killing of the buffalo was a spiritual tragedy."

David looked at Dale with an unspoken question in his eyes. Dale answered David's thought, "The buffalo was like a god. It's hard to explain. The buffalo gave us food and shelter as a gift. The buffalo was part of Indian culture and thought."

The three men sat in silence for a few moments, sipping their drinks and thinking about Dale's statement.

David made his own contribution to the conversation. "What you just said reminds me of what is going on in Alaska today."

"How?" Dale asked. Lester looked up and watched with renewed respect for David as he listened to his explanation.

"The Gwitch'in Athabascan Indians in Northern Alaska depend on the migration of the Porcupine Caribou herd for food and shelter. They, too, talk about the spiritual importance of the

Caribou to their lives and culture. They are concerned the activities of the oil companies on the Arctic Slope might damage the calving grounds of the herd."

"Don't the oil companies have enough oil up there without going where the caribou migrate?" Dale asked with obvious irritation at still another intrusion into a Native culture.

David answered, "I guess oil companies want more. The company officials say they 'need to know' where the oil is just in case there is another Middle East embargo or whatever. The problem is, if people 'know' there is oil available, they always find a need to exploit it."

"It's hard for people to know there is a resource worth millions within their grasp and not take it, especially for white men," Lester said.

"I hate to disagree with you, but even non-whites get greedy these days," David answered. "We got off the subject, though, Lester. You were telling us about the Fort Laramie treaty."

Lester continued his story. "Chief Red Cloud led the warriors into a battle to regain control of our lands and force the U.S. government to negotiate the treaty of Ft. Laramie. It was signed in 1868 and supposedly promised us all the Black Hills and western South Dakota." Lester reached for a book from the shelf to show David the confirmation. of his facts. "Whites were forbidden to enter land set aside as Lakota. Red Cloud and his followers finally settled by the Fort because the buffalo were getting scarce."

Lester paused, and Dale took up the history lesson. "Crazy Horse was another warrior you've probably heard about. He stayed on the traditional hunting grounds and refused to sign the treaty with the government."

David interjected another question.

"Yes, I've heard about Crazy Horse. Wasn't he murdered by some of his followers or something?"

Lester replied, "Yes, he was. After the treaty was signed, whites discovered gold and the government pressured the Lakota to change the terms of the treaty. Crazy Horse refused," Lester's pride in this warrior was evident in his voice. "He was the one who led the battle against Custer at the Little Big Horn in 1876. The government was so shocked by Custer's defeat they were willing to do anything to get rid of him and his band."

David smiled as he recalled, "You know the government was still calling the Battle of the Little Big Horn the Custer Massacre until a few years ago."

Lester said, "It's a massacre when the whites lose, but a battle when the Indians lose." Lester got up from the table as he spoke and went to the refrigerator for more beers.

Dale continued to tell the story, "About a year later, Crazy Horse and his followers had to surrender because the buffalo were so scarce the people were beginning to starve." Dale pulled on one of his braids as he talked. "He was killed by white soldiers and Indian police. Nobody knows where he is buried, but we think it is near here."

David asked, "Why would the Indians want to kill him?"

Dale tried to explain.

"It goes back to Red Cloud and Crazy Horse. Each wanted to keep the land but they had different ways of dealing with the white men. Red Cloud thought it would be better to negotiate the best settlement they could get." Dale looked at Lester, who nodded in agreement. "Crazy Horse didn't think you could sell the land or negotiate it away because it would be like selling your mother."

Lester continued, "How to deal with the white man has been a problem ever since. There have been differences of opinion right up to Wounded Knee."

David asked, "You mean the massacre at Wounded Knee?"

Lester gestured with his hand in a way which reminded David of a trial lawyer arguing a case before a jury. "You must be thinking of the last massacre in the 1890's where over three hundred of our people were slaughtered by soldiers. They are buried in a mass grave." He stared into the air, sadness written on his face.

Dale said, "Lester means the second one. It was back in the 1970's when another 60 of our people were killed in civil warfare between the American Indian Movement and the government sponsored goon squads."

"Who in the government sponsored them?" David asked in disbelief.

"The FBI and our own BIA," Dale said, his anger betrayed by the grimace on his face.

"Are those kinds of tensions still here on the reservation?" David asked.

"There are always some disagreements on what we should do to get back our land and control of our lives," Lester answered with a hint of anger in his voice. "Over the last couple of decades there's been some healing. Some of the bureaucrats even see the importance of right and just action."

He paused thoughtfully, then continued with an example. "You know the Supreme Court admitted the stealing of the Black Hills was reprehensible. Those were their words." He held up a legal binder which contained a copy of the court ruling. "A couple of senators and representatives have introduced bills into Congress to help us get it back."

Lester paused again before adding in a louder voice, "We will someday. I guarantee it."

David thought the promise was shrouded in a threat, creating a tension in the room which seemed to hang like a shadow over the table for the next few minutes.

David tried to ease the tension by joking with Lester as he said, "You sound like you have found your mission in life."

Lester gave him a serious look. "I have, my friend."

Dale also sought to lift Lester's mood and changed the subject. He said to David, "I hate to break up the history lesson, but if you're going to make your phone calls, you better do it before it's too late."

"Thanks," David said. "I was so interested in this conversation, I completely forgot about the calls I need to make. Could I use your phone, Lester?"

"It's on the desk over there," Lester replied. "Help yourself."

Chapter 14

David dialed the number of his hotel and asked the desk operator if there were any messages for him. Holly and Ward had called him. It was expected. Someone else had, too. But there was no name or number to return the call. So he was still being watched.

Holly wasn't home. He was relieved. He didn't know what he would tell her anyway.

He wasn't any more sure about what to tell Ward, but at least he knew there was danger, and after all, David had promised to keep in touch. He could at least report that he was still alive, if not completely well.

"I'm still here," David said quietly when Ward answered the phone.

"I was able to confirm your suspicions about your meeting," Ward said. "My source in Washington says the man you were going to meet was the same one who was killed at Mount Rushmore. He doesn't know much else, but suspects there may be more to the story. We both think you may be getting into something dangerous."

"Yeah, I know," David admitted. He knew already there was more to this than mere danger. "The people here have been watched as well. I think the military or the CIA, or somebody, is up to its eyeballs in something here. We were followed by a black helicopter as we drove out to the reservation today, and my companions say this is not an isolated event. They are seeing a lot of these things out here."

David noticed the receiver was wet and realized he had broken into a cold sweat. He had known his suspicions were correct, but it gave him a jolt to have them confirmed.

"There's something else, Ward," David added.

"What is it?" Ward asked.

"I think I'm sick," David stated. "I've been fainting or something. I think I'm losing my mind at times. I'm sweating and can't understand why. I think I'm losing touch with reality." David felt sick as he admitted the fear that returned to overwhelm him.

Ward was silent. The pause seemed to last an eternity.

"I don't like this, David. I think you better come back home and forget this assignment. We'll send someone else out," he suggested.

It was David's turn to pause. "No, I can't do that, Ward. I have to see this out. I'd be running away if I came home now."

"But you said yourself that you are sick. We can't have you trying to function out there in that condition. You have to get well," Ward insisted.

"No, Ward. I'm ok, really. This will pass, I'm sure. It's important to me to see this through,"

"Ok, but if you change your mind...." Ward let the option drop.

David changed the subject to ease his mind. "I spent the day out here on the Indian reservation."

"What were you doing out there?" Ward asked. "Were you up at the testing site?"

"Not yet," David answered. "We are going out there tomorrow."

"I take it 'we' are the same people who have seen the helicopters?" Ward asked, with obvious interest.

"Yeah, Indian friends from the Reservation," David answered. "I should be back at the hotel tomorrow. We should talk about how I am to get to Gallup to look up the information in the safety deposit box."

"I've made the reservations. Ticket should be at the airline counter. Pick it up when you get back to town," Ward explained.

David hung up the phone plagued by the sense of being watched. He turned and noticed Dale and Lester looking at him in puzzled silence. David walked to the table and accepted a beer from Dale. He had already decided his two new friends could be trusted with anything he had to say.

Dale said, "Are you feeling ok? You still look pale."

David knew he had been unable to suppress his anxiety and the two men had sensed it.

"I'm fine," David said. "I guess you must have heard I'm going to Gallup."

"We heard," Lester responded for both friends. "Mind if I ask what you are planning to do there?"

"Quite frankly, I'd like you to know," David answered. "It has to do with work."

Dale looked at him in surprise. He could not make out what a trip to Gallup had to do with the events David had told him about.

David explained, "Dale knows a little about my assignment. I was sent out to meet a man. He was supposed to give me information about the weapons testing facility near here. It has some kind of cover as a Hollywood production center. We never met, and my boss just confirmed my suspicions about why." David glanced at Dale and said, "He was the man, Dale, who was killed at Mount Rushmore yesterday."

Dale and Lester looked at each other, their expressions showing a new understanding of seemingly unrelated events.

Lester spoke first. "We knew about the murder. We've been tailing those responsible. Our group suspected it had something to do with weapons tests, but we weren't sure."

Dale added, "We were sure about who pushed the man over the Cliff."

David said, "Dale told me a little about your work here, and the attempts to get your land back." He looked at Lester. "Can you tell me more?"

Lester paused, then began to tell about the operation.

"There is a loose organization of us here who have been following some shady activities on the military base next to the reservation. It started with the land problem, which you've already heard a little about. We became involved because of our desire to regain our land."

Dale shuffled and moved closer to the table. He spoke in hushed tones, as if he was trying to keep any uninvited being from hearing what he had to say.

"We have plants inside," he said confidentially.

"Plants?" David repeated, seeking an explanation.

"They are our friends and our spies, mostly Indian brothers and sisters. They gather information for us," Dale said. "They have jobs on the base. Over the past couple of years, they have been able to tell us what this facility is doing with taxpayers' money. You wouldn't believe what's going on."

David was interested in hearing more. He leaned forward over the table, and the three men looked like conspirators making their plans.

Lester continued, "We've found out about some secret weapons testing. It sounds bizarre. One report I read called it 'global vandalism'."

David listened intently. "What are they doing to reach global proportions?" he asked.

Lester explained, "The project disturbs parts of the atmosphere without splitting atoms or building bombs. The physicists are looking into how they can use electro-magnetism to change the density, temperature, and structure of the ionosphere."

"I don't understand," David admitted. "How does that create global vandalism?"

Lester attempted to describe the goals of the research. "Apparently, the idea is to find a way to control global weather patterns, disrupt world communications, destroy enemy missiles in space, and even affect people's moods or mental functions." He rose and walked in agitation around the room as he talked. "They could change natural migration patterns of fish or birds or other animals which rely on geomagnetic fields to help them find their directions."

Lester looked grim as he described the project. David began to understand the importance of it only a little at a time. "How can it affect so many different things," he asked.

"We don't understand how they plan to do it exactly, only what the possibilities are according to those scientists putting it together. From what our plants have uncovered, they are testing how animals and people, even air safety and radio transmissions are affected by the projection of energy from these huge antennae." He sat back down and leaned over the table. "You see, we are among their guinea pigs. It's more than land we have to worry about now."

"Yes," added Dale, who looked as serious as Lester. "Our future is at stake. We don't know what this might do to our health, our children's health, the health of the animals who live here."

"Indians aren't the only ones who will be affected by this, though. Everyone who lives near here is a test subject for these mad scientists and power hungry generals," Lester said. "It's like the tests the government ran on citizens in Minnesota in the 1950's when they decided to see what effects some kind of gas would have on humans."

"The same kind of thing happened in Nevada and Utah with some of the nuclear tests, too," Dale added. "Indians usually get the worst of it, because they are the ones living in the isolated regions of the west."

"I remember reading about farmers and city people around southern Utah having high cancer and leukemia rates," David added.

"It's true, as I said, Indians aren't the only ones to be affected, as I just said," Lester said.

"What do you think they are after here?" David realized why someone might not want him to uncover information like this, and that they would probably kill to prevent him from finding out about it.

"From all we know so far," Lester explained, "it looks like they want to be able to control the amount of ultra-violet radiation people are exposed to, and change bird migrations and jet streams. If they had this kind of power, they could take over radio navigation signals, even electronic devices like pacemakers and computers. They could wipe out the banking system and create economic havoc."

"I guess if they really could control all those important areas, they would have ultimate power," David admitted. "Do you think they can really do it?"

"I don't know, but I don't want to assume they can't," Lester said. "We haven't been able to do anything about it yet. We're not talking to anyone about it, but we've been watching them through our plants. I don't think the people up at the facility know about us."

Dale disagreed. "I'm not so sure they don't know about us. If they can use the FBI and CIA and any other intelligence network, they wouldn't have any trouble checking up on a bunch of radical Indians, as government types like to refer to us. I think the facility people don't care at the moment because we aren't any danger to them right now. It might change since the explosion of the experimental craft they sent up."

"You might be right," Lester had to admit.

"What do they have to do with the explosion?" David sought more answers. He continued to reconstruct the events of the past few days taking into account the new information he was receiving now. The pieces were starting to fit together.

"Facility people were involved with the crash, according to our plants. We were able to get to the site before the official investigation did." Lester rose from the table and disappeared briefly. He reentered the room carrying a charred black rectangular box.

"We found this," Lester's voice sounded dry and calm, but his shaking hands betrayed his nervousness.

"What is it?" David was fascinated by the object placed on the table before them.

"We don't know for sure," Lester said. "It is supposed to have some data in it, and our plants told us what to look for at the site. Our plants don't want 'The Colonels' out at the facility to get it back until we know what's in it."

Dale said, "Our plants told us the craft or whatever it was belonged to 'The Colonels.' They tell us this operation was so secret other branches of the military were not supposed to know about it. The facility people weren't happy that this weapon was the one falling out of the sky and announcing itself to the world."

"Do you have any idea why it crashed?" David asked.

"The plants have an idea," Dale said. "You will probably think we are crazy. It sounds crazy every time I say it."

Dale stopped talking. He and Lester looked at each other, and shifted uncomfortably in their chairs. Neither seemed to want to go on. David prodded them to keep telling him what they knew.

"You believe in UFO's?" Lester asked tentatively.

"Dunno," David said quite truthfully. "Why, what does it have to do with all this?"

"This is nuts," Dale said, shaking his head, "but it's real."

There was a long silence as they sat sipping beers, each waiting for another to speak.

"We've been seeing a lot of strange stuff around here," Lester started to explain. "They aren't just northern lights, either. We know northern lights when we see them."

Dale nodded in agreement and added, "We believe that facility down there has a Hollywood cover for a reason."

"Why would Hollywood have anything to do with weapons testing?" David asked.

"It has to do with propaganda," Lester said.

"For what? Who are they trying to convince, and of what?" David asked.

"The public is the target. Why do you think there has been such an increase in alien-related subjects for television and movies? It's a way of making people accept something they wouldn't believe otherwise." Lester declared.

"So you think that Hollywood is being used to influence people's beliefs?" David asked.

"Sure. Remember how Hollywood used to show Indians. John Wayne was always leading the cavalry charges against us murderous savages. Because of that, people thought all we could say was 'ugh, killum whiteman.' Now, we're the good guys, thanks to Kevin Costner and Marlon Brando and a few others. At least they have us closer to the truth."

"I still don't see how that has anything to do with a weapons-testing facility." David admitted.

"Because Hollywood is getting its special effects, and the military is getting its money to test new equipment under an umbrella of the movie industry and corporate interests," Dale said.

"Ok, there have been stranger bedfellows, I'll admit. But what is this about UFO's, then?" David asked.

"We've seen 'em. There's something out here and the military doesn't want us to know. They're working together — all of them." Lester said.

"Who is?" David was still confused.

"The military, CIA, corporate America, and fantasy land." Lester said.

"Fantasy land?" David queried.

"You know, dream makers, Hollywood. A whole industry that is intent on confusing make-believe and reality. They can twist your mind in so many directions that you don't know what is real and what isn't. What better cover for the military than that?" Dale said.

David knew he was right. "Ok, I'll buy that. So tell me more."

"We've had a lot of unexplained sightings around here. Strange lights and sounds. Aircraft that don't behave like any we've seen before. All those black helicopters. Some people who have reported things to officials have been visited by authorities who tell them they haven't seen anything at all. Cattle mutilations. Crop circles. We've had it all." Lester explained.

Dale continued, "The day that craft exploded, we watched an aerial dogfight like you've never seen. It was like a war up there, and one or more shot that thing out of the sky. It didn't just crash by accident."

"Yeah, and those lights, they were having a battle, too. It's like some were on one side, and some on another. One of those crashed, too." Lester added.

David could make no sense of any of this. These were intelligent men, obviously disturbed by something they had seen. But he, himself, had experiences the past couple of days he could neither understand nor explain either. Something very serious was wrong, but he didn't know what it was or what he could do about it.

Dale continued, "The debris scattered over a wide area. We were lucky to find this."

David asked, "Why weren't the facility people out looking for it sooner?"

Lester answered, "I don't think 'The Colonels' believed it survived. After they realized some other pieces had, they mounted a major search all over the region looking for this. It might not take them long to figure out we're the ones who have it."

David thought out loud as he looked at the puzzle pieces in his head. "You think the craft, some kind of secret weapon, was sent up by a clique of military personnel testing electro-magnetic pulses and their ability to alter the ionosphere. Some UFO knocked the weapon out of orbit. My contact must have known, but was killed before he could tell me. You were following the murderer, and they've been following me."

The silence was almost like a blanket settling over the table. David looked up to see Lester and Dale staring at him, still as stone. He realized what he had said and what it implied for them.

"If they are following me, now they will connect me with you," he said dryly. His stomach turned over, as he thought of the danger in which all three of them had been placed.

"How do you know you are being followed?" Lester asked, hoping to reach some other conclusion.

"I had a strange call on the airport paging phone just as I arrived in Rapid City. The man never identified himself. He only said he knew why I was there and I was being watched. After the man was killed, the same person called my room. He knew my meeting had not taken place and why."

Dale added, "We were followed today, too. One of the black helicopters."

Lester and Dale looked again at one another. Lester explained, "There's something else we should tell you."

David watched Lester struggle with the words. It was odd to see this man, usually so adept at conversation, at a loss for words. Lester spoke in short choppy sentences as he thought of ways to introduce the impossible to David.

"It's bizarre. There are these strangers. It's weird. We think they have something to do with all this."

"What kind of strangers," David asked.

Lester continued, a bit more composed. "Our plants down at the facility. They say there are a group of 'people' that don't seem real."

"What do you mean, not real?" David asked.

"These are different. They don't seem human. They look human, they walk and talk. But there is something missing. There's something wrong with them." Dale said.

"How can anyone tell?" David asked.

"Just a feeling, I guess. You know how a dog can read your personality? It's kind of the same thing. But they seem to be in control of the weapons tests down there. They are working with the military or CIA or whoever is there on the government side of operation." Lester said.

Dale's foot tapped nervously against the table leg. Lester was staring down at his hands, tightly clasped in front of him, as David fiddled with a spoon.

After what seemed like the passage of hours to David, Dale continued to speak. "We think they are plants, too, like our plants in the complex. These must be plants for someone out of this world. We don't know what to call them, or how to describe them. We just call them 'Plants'."

"How do you know if you see one?" David asked.

Lester answered, "You might not. They seem like humans until you've been around them awhile. We're beginning to think the craft was hit by a UFO trying to contact or retrieve one of it's own plants, or else one group was trying to prevent another from getting the thing into orbit."

"What do you think they want here?" David asked. "There must be some scientific explanation for this."

Lester and Dale began to chuckle. They looked at each other and in unison began to sing "Do-do-do-do, Do-do-do-do" to the tune of the theme from "The Twilight Zone." It was obvious to David these two must often break into such humorous antics. Somehow, it helped break the tension of the conversation to see that in spite of everything, these two could still retain their humor.

Dale became serious again before he answered, "Look, David. I don't know what to believe, but I can tell you Indians have always believed in things white men didn't seem to see."

David knew Dale was right. He nodded in agreement.

"I'm not an Indian, but this white man saw some things in Alaska I would never have believed if I hadn't seen them myself," he added. "To say nothing of today."

Dale continued, "Maybe there are other things we are being shown we haven't seen before. Something can be real although it hasn't been published in the most current science journal."

Lester added, "Indians sense spirits in a way most white men have lost because they closed their eyes to them. Maybe science hasn't discovered everything about the universe. We should keep our eyes open. We can only tell you what our plants have told us, and what we have seen ourselves."

David agreed. Dale said, "We have men like Sam Going Away. They have more insight into these things than we'll ever have. Men like Sam have mystical and mythical powers. You know, he told me men like him flew to the moon long before white men made rocket ships."

"This is the second time in a week I've been told about flights to the moon." David could not control his growing excitement. He had nearly lost the fear which had so overwhelmed him in the past few days.

"What were you told the first time?" Lester asked.

David explained, "I was at an art gallery the other night in L.A. I met an Eskimo artist there. He told me how he used to hear stories of the shamans who would fly to the moon."

"Yes," Lester agreed, "there are many similarities among Native American cultures and traditions."

David brought the conversation back to the mysterious object on the table in front of them.

"What are you going to do with this now? Why don't you take it to the papers. I could write a story on it."

Lester looked at Dale, then at David.

"We need your help, but not in the way you think," Lester said. "We don't want to end up like our Sioux brother, Leonard Peltier. He's been sitting in jail for a murder back at Wounded Knee he says he didn't commit. We know enough about how the government responded to the Wounded Knee uprising to approach this differently. We might be considered radicals, but we're going to be quiet radicals."

"What do you plan to do?" David prodded.

"We're not sure yet," Dale said. "We'll keep using our plants to find out what the scientists and military are doing. We don't want the government to find out what we know. We'd rather have them think we aren't interested in them, either."

"We want you to be part of our efforts," Lester said. "When the time is right, the story will have to be told. We will want you to write this then, but not now. We think some of our plants can help us get the information held in this box."

David felt a rush of excitement and pride. "When I come back from Gallup, we'll see what steps to take next. I'll do whatever I can to help."

The three men nodded in agreement and toasted to their future success and friendship.

The night was late and the day had been long. The topics turned to something more lighthearted, college stories and Indian jokes. When David settled down to sleep on Lester's couch, it was well past 3:00 a.m.

Dale was already asleep in a bag on the floor. His snoring did not interrupt David's racing thoughts. He saw the beams of silvery light cast upon the floor. David rose and walked to the window where he could see the moon peeking between the branches of a tree, and thought he could see within it the profile of an old Indian's head, confirming one of Lester's stories. He returned to the couch and closed his eyes and drifted off with thoughts of floating aliens and exploding stars.

Chapter 15

The friends rose early the next morning to prepare for their excursion to the crash site. Lester fried eggs and pancakes. David awoke smelling the aromas of coffee and sausage. Seemed strange that such different odors could combine into such an appealing scent. The three men shared the substantial breakfast, after which all three men piled into Dale's pickup. Lester whistled, and three dogs came bounding around the corner of the house. They greeted Lester and his friends with excitement and jumped into the back of the vehicle.

The dogs' excitement reflected that of the men, who experienced the rush of adrenaline naturally present in any dangerous or clandestine activity. One man, they knew, had been killed because of his interest or knowledge about the area they were preparing to trespass. It was possible they might be discovered, too, especially if David was being watched.

Lester explained the secret nature of the site to David.

"This does not officially exist, except as a Hollywood production facility. The military would never admit they have anything to do with its operations. No one would ever admit to testing weapons here." Lester said as he rolled down the window of the passenger's seat.

David, squeezed in the middle of the seat, tried to position his legs so they would not interfere with the gearshift. The pickup roared as it lurched over ruts and bumps. David almost had to yell to make himself heard as he responded to Lester's comment.

"It sounds like the government is denying their involvement here just as surely as they deny the existence of some of their military bases. Like the one in Nevada. I can't remember the name of it, but it's one of the secret bases they say isn't there at all."

Lester yelled above the engine, "I've heard about it, too. From what I've heard, ufologists claim it is so secret because it is conducting UFO research. Maybe they are denying any involvement here for some of the same reasons."

Dale shifted down and added, "We know about this place because of our ancestral ties to this land. We grew up around here and know the country. Besides, they took some of our land to build the facility, and used some of our people as the labor force."

David asked, "Wasn't it risky to have local people know about any military involvement here if they wanted to keep it a secret?"

Lester yelled his answer, "They must have thought using Reservation Indians would be the best they could do. I think they assumed Indians would be happy to have a job."

Lester lurched into David and back against the door as the pickup hit a large rock. He apologized and continued his explanation, "Reservation Indians are already separate from off-reservation people, so they probably believed there was less opportunity for talk. It opened up the possibility for us to put our plants in the facility, though."

The road narrowed to a mere wagon path and the pickup slowed to a crawl. After over an hour of bumpy and jerky ride, they arrived at the upper edge of a deep canyon. Dale shut off the engine, and the three men walked to the rim.

"From here, we go on foot," Dale said.

The three men stood at the cliff edge as the dogs cavorted on the grass behind them. Lester removed a pair of binoculars from his pocket and scanned the hills in the distance.

"It's over there, about five miles away," Lester said as he pointed the way.

"What is over there, the base?" David asked.

"No, the crash site," Lester said.

David looked toward the horizon, following the direction indicated by Lester's outstretched hand. David became aware of a mechanical sound in the distance gradually getting louder.

"What's the noise?" he asked.

"I hear it, too," Dale said. "It sounds like a chopper. Can you see anything, Lester?"

David sensed some alarm in Dale's voice. Lester scanned the horizon and the sky above it with the binoculars. His voice was more calm than Dale's, but David thought Lester was also tense.

"I'm not sure what is going on," Lester responded to Dale's question. "I think I see ATV's or four-wheelers out there, but I'm not certain what they are. I don't see anything in the sky, but I hear a chopper."

The helicopter surprised them by its sudden appearance over the hill behind them. The echoes of sound bouncing from the hills and walls of the canyons had deceptively distorted recognition of the direction from which the aircraft approached. It rose behind the men and swooped down over them like a hawk pursuing mice before they could react. The shadow of the great mechanical bird swept beyond them and continued to darken a path on the ground leading to the site of the crash.

The dogs howled and ran in circles around the pickup as if to encourage the men to flee. Dale gasped, "We better get out of here."

All three ran back to the pickup and piled in. Dale raced the motor to life, and they began to retrace the bumpy trail.

Lester spoke for them all. "I don't think today is a good day to go exploring. They must have seen us. Maybe they don't know what we were doing here, but I don't think we want to stay and find out."

"We'll try again when you come back from New Mexico," Dale told David as they bounced and jolted along the grassy dirt path.

"We know what they are looking for, and we have it," Lester added. "Their investigation cannot take long, because they aren't going to find anything. I hope they didn't get a good look at the pickup."

David observed, "It wouldn't matter now, anyway. If they found you from following me, they already know what to look for." His palms were sweaty and he could feel his pulse pounding at his neck and wrists. He hated to think he might be responsible for placing others in jeopardy.

"Look, David," Dale yelled over the engine as he shifted gears, "Don't worry about us. It's not your fault."

David thought Dale had read his thoughts. He said, "I am the one they were following."

Lester agreed with Dale. "We are in this, too. They may have known about us all along. We will deal with the problems as they come to us."

None of them had much to say during the journey back to Lester's house. David thought the trip back was somehow longer, but he knew it was because they were all preoccupied and tense. The trip seemed endless to David, but at long last they arrived at Lester's house. The distant rumble of helicopter engines greeted them as they emerged from the pickup. Lester pointed out two craft hovering in the distance. It seemed to David the helicopters were watching them, waiting to learn the men's destination. The craft turned and disappeared over the horizon.

David read the concern in the glances passed between Dale and Lester. He had no need to ask the reason for their apprehension.

"You think they followed us?" Dale asked Lester.

"Probably," Lester said. "They could have taken pictures or followed us so they would know where to find us."

Dale and David accompanied Lester to the door. The trip back to town would take some time, and Dale suggested they start soon.

"If the military is following us, we should get on the road anyway," Dale said. "We don't want them watching Lester's house because the pickup is here."

David agreed. Lester gave David the telephone number of his friend, Joe Gaagii, in the southwest.

"Contact him when you get to Gallup," Lester instructed David, "and he will take you out to Sam's friend Charlie. Charlie has the package Sam wants you to bring back to him."

David and Dale returned to town in tense silence. Dale dropped David at his hotel.

"Good luck in Gallup," Dale said as David departed. "Keep in touch."

"Watch out for yourself, too," David grasped Dale's hand through the driver's window. He felt sad, like he was saying good-bye for the last time to someone who had become a good friend and colleague.

David went to his room, exhausted. He tossed restlessly as in his mind, he ran along canyon rims chased by something he could not see. He fell, with Lester and Dale, into dark bottomless chasms. In all his dreams, he could hear the rhythmic roar of the helicopter hovering above him.

Julian St. Germaine waited impatiently for Col. Losskey's arrival. The latest glitch in the operation disturbed him. It should not have happened.

The Colonel stepped into St. Germaine's expansive GALCOM office. Through the window, the Seattle skyline glimmered in a rare sunny morning.

"What is this report all about?" St. Germaine demanded.

"We're on it, sir. Just a slight setback. We don't know how the Aurora went down yet. Our people are working on it." Losskey declared confidently.

"Your people!" St. Germaine's disdain was obvious. "What happened?"

"It was shot down." Losskey admitted.

"I suspected as much. Why didn't you just say that in the first place." St. Germaine stared down his long, straight nose. "You know I don't have to keep feeding your little experiments on the ozone layer."

"Look," the Colonel replied, "we need each other. Let's just try to work together here." It wasn't easy working with this arrogant being, he thought. Losskey had dealt with many unpleasant men in his life, but never had he met one as arrogant and controlling as St. Germaine. He hoped he could get transferred out of this arrangement, but it wasn't likely. There was just too much at stake now. If things were successful, he'd be on easy street. If not, then nothing would matter anyway.

"Who did it?" St. Germaine asked.

"The usual suspects," Losskey replied. St. Germaine accepted this enigmatic statement without comment.

"Did we have any success with the test before it was destroyed?" he asked instead.

"We think so. And we got one of them." Losskey. "Well, we almost have him."

"What is that supposed to mean," St. Germaine asked with a sneer.

"We shot one of them down. He has escaped for the moment, but we know he is on the reservation. We're watching the renegade Indians down there. He can't go anywhere. We'll have him soon," Losskey promised.

"Your words don't mean much if you can't produce the results," St. Germaine declared. "What about this?" He asked, holding up another report.

"He's a reporter. We don't know if he has any connection to this or not. He was going to meet Rosenburg, but we took care of that. This Seabird has been snooping around the Reservation, but he's not going to find anything," Losskey explained.

"He'd better not," St. Germaine threatened.

Chapter 16

David was awakened from his troubled sleep by the ringing of the phone. The wake-up call jarred him into activity. He arrived at the airport early and absently watched the people moving through the terminal, preoccupied by the events of the past few days. Years might have elapsed since he left California for all he knew. This week had changed him forever.

David passed through the security gate and sat at the boarding gate to wait for his flight. Within a few minutes, two men approached him. Dressed in dark suits and ties, they carried themselves with professional authority.

"Mr. Seabird," the tall man with a long face and thin, graying hair addressed him by name. "We must ask you to come with us."

"Why?" David had no intention of going with any stranger.

"We are with security," the second man explained. He was short and stocky with a bald head. David looked at them and was reminded of Mutt and Jeff. His answer was disdainful.

"I've been through security." He continued to remain seated.

"We'll explain if you come with us." The two men had not expected resistance from David. The tall one shuffled his feet, betraying to David a crack in the authoritative and confident facade.

"You can explain it to me here," David remained unmoved. His confidence increased, while the men's seemed to wither under David's resistance and apparent lack of fear of or respect for their authority. David was by now certain they were not who they claimed to be.

"We can't explain it here. It's a confidential matter." The shorter man spoke in a strained voice.

"I'm not going anywhere with you," David said flatly. "If you think I'm guilty of something, then arrest me. Otherwise, I'm getting on my flight."

David raised his voice in irritation, deliberately calling attention to the men who spoke with him. They, too, noticed the other passengers had lowered their voices or stopped their own conversations to watch the developing altercation.

The strangers looked at each other and the short man pulled the taller one out of David's earshot. They conversed briefly and the tall man disappeared down the concourse. The shorter one stood near a pillar, watching David as he continued to wait, pretending not to notice. A few minutes later, the tall man returned with a paper which he showed to the short man.

They conversed for a few minutes, then the tall man walked over to David.

"We apologize for the inconvenience," he said. "We seem to have made an error. Have a good flight to Gallup."

David felt his lip twitch. They knew where he was going. This flight was destined for Denver, where he was to change airplanes. He tried not to look shaken. He could not tell if he succeeded. The men stood against the wall across from the concourse, watching him until he boarded the flight.

David gazed out the window watching the cloud patterns during the flight. He was caught up in his thoughts, and unaware of the passage of time. He realized, with slight surprise, the plane was approaching Denver, and the flight was nearly over. David toyed with the idea of changing his ticket. He was troubled by the fact the men in the airport seemed to know his every move. Perhaps he should wait to go to Gallup, and spend a few days in a nearby hotel. He could return to L.A. and go to Gallup from there.

David considered his choices as he walked through the concourse, half realizing he was looking around for someone watching or following him. He decided he was giving in to paranoia. In any case, if these people knew his plans, they could also find out the changes in them. There was no running away from the danger. He would continue on to Gallup.

When David arrived, his first action was to call Joe Gaagii from his cell phone.

"Lester and Dale say hello." David said into the receiver.

"Any friend of theirs is a friend of mine," Joe said, happy to remember good times with his northern brothers.

"Where do you need to go?" Joe asked.

"Can you take me to see Sam's friend, Charlie? He is supposed to have something for me."

"Sure, be happy to. He lives out past Window Rock. You gonna get wheels?" Joe asked.

"Yeah, I've booked a car," David replied. "If you give me directions, I can drive out there tomorrow."

"Better yet, I'll go out with you," Joe offered.

"Great. How should we arrange it? I have to check out a couple of things here in town today," David explained.

"Come and get me tomorrow when you are ready to leave town. Here's where I live." Joe said.

After writing down the instructions Joe dictated, David clicked off the phone, picked up his bag, and rented his car. He drove directly to the bank and asked for entry to the safety deposit box he had been instructed to see.

Once inside, he opened the box to find a single sealed envelope. He removed it and carefully opened it. The letter within was typed, and only hinted at what the man might have told him had they met face to face.

"The fact you are reading this letter indicates I have been killed. You have become involved in a very dangerous operation, and it will be impossible for you to know who you can trust and who you cannot. As a scientific researcher at a classified military complex, I had access to information about disturbing and extreme projects being tested. This reaches to the highest levels of the government. The Pentagon is involved. The CIA is involved. You probably will not be able to confirm any of this, however, because they will stop you, just as they stopped me.

"The experiments have global implications. Not only will they level destructive forces against the environment. The creatures running these tests which will channel energy as a weapon, destroy the ozone layer, and cause other irreversible atmospheric destruction, are using human subjects without their prior consent, and if successful, will consolidate power in the hands of a few people devoid of any moral constraints. Had I survived, I would have given you as much help as possible. You must now rely on my colleague." The letter gave a name and phone number. The last sentence was a warning: "We have never before in history faced a crisis like this. Paul Rosenburg."

David carefully folded the letter and placed it in his pocket. As he left the vault, his hands were shaking. What could Rosenburg have meant, a crisis the like of which had never been seen before. There had been many great crises in history — what could be more than wars, persecutions, all that the world had been through. He couldn't shake the fear that gripped him, but kept telling himself that Rosenburg was exaggerating the situation.

He drove to a mall where he could use a public phone, suddenly aware of the fact that his conversations on his cell phone might be monitored by someone watching him. He dialed the number given in the letter.

"Hello." The voice of the woman who answered was soothing and accented.

"I would like to speak to Karl Baden, please," David said. There was no response.

"Hello," David repeated. "Hello, is anyone there?"

"Who is dis?" The woman's voice was abrupt and tense, almost suspicious.

"My name is David Seabird," David said gently.

"I do not know any David Seabird," the woman responded.

There was another period of silence, but the woman did not hang up. David heard her ask, "Who are you? Vat do you vahnt?"

"I was told to contact Dr. Baden," David replied.

"Who told you to talk to him?" she demanded.

"Paul Rosenburg." David clenched his teeth as he voiced the name of the man he had seen at the bottom of the cliff at Mount Rushmore. There was a long silence as David waited for the woman to respond.

When she finally spoke, David realized she way crying.

"Paul told you to talk to Karl? How does he know you?" The woman asked her questions between sobs.

"He gave me Dr. Baden's name and number in a letter." David was confused by the woman's response, and disturbed.

"He has died," the woman said through her tears.

"I know, it's why I have the letter," David said. His revelation was followed by a long silence. The woman quit crying, in shock. When she spoke, her voice was so faint David had trouble hearing her words.

"Paul, too?" the thin, frail voice said.

David was stunned as he realized the implications of her words.

"I'm so sorry," he said. "I thought you were talking about Paul. I did not know about Dr. Baden. Can you tell me what happened?"

She was cautious. "How do I know I can trust you?"

David explained his role in the events of the past few days. When she heard his story, she expressed her willingness to talk to him.

"We can meet in the park. Can you go there in one hour?" she said, adding the instructions for getting there.

He was tired and shaken, but he did not want to postpone any meeting with Mrs. Baden. David went to the park and sat on a bench, trying to calm his fear by watching the pigeons. Instead, he found himself watching the people, wondering which one of them was following him and ready to snuff out his life as easily as killing some broken-winged pigeon.

An older woman sat on the bench beside him, assessing him closely. After an exchange of greetings based on the descriptions they had given one another, David knew this was the woman he had spoken to over the phone.

Mrs. Baden must have been beautiful when she was young. She was still a striking and lovely woman with graying blond hair and Germanic features.

"Mr. Seabird," she said gently in a German accent, "I am sorry I was so rude to you. It is such a shock, you see. I did not think someone vould call for Karl now."

"I'm the one who should apologize," David said with sincerity. "I did not mean to cause you pain. I just had no idea your husband had died recently. Can you tell me what happened?"

"They say to me his brakes are no good," she said, her eyes downcast. "His car could not make a curve on the mountain. He died two weeks ago. I think he has been killed. I think, Paul, too, must be killed by the same men."

"Yes, I suspect you are right. I want to find out who did this. Will you help me with any information you might have?" David asked, already feeling that action would help calm his own fears.

"Yes, I am grateful to you," she admitted. "I will give you anything I have of Karl's. I know it vill not bring Karl back to me, but I might know vat happened to him. Why vould someone vant to kill him?" Her eyes filled with pools of tears as she spoke.

"Why do you think he was killed?" David gently prodded.

"I see him change. Six or eight months ago, he is depressed. He seems depressed ven he is usually not a man to vorry. He acts afraid then," she answered.

"Was he afraid of anything or anyone in particular?" David asked.

"I do not know," the woman answered. "I know he and Paul vork on something together. Both seem afraid and think they are followed by someone."

"Do you think they were being followed?" David pressed for more information.

"Yes, I think they believed so. Karl changed other vays, too," she said.

"Can you explain what you mean?" David asked.

"I think he believes something vill happen to him. He brings me flowers and cards. Karl always had our German reserve. This is not like him," She smiled slightly as she remembered tender moments with her husband. She began to sob again.

"This is vhy I think he expected to be killed," she wept. "He is very afraid for both of us. He knew he was going to die soon," she continued. "There are men around our house some days."

"What men," David asked.

"Before Karl died, men in cars near our house. They are all in dark cars and dark clothes. Their eyes are covered with dark glasses, even when the day is cloudy. Karl sees them and he is afraid," she explained.

David knew how Dr. Baden had felt. He, too, was feeling the fear of being watched, of having others know what you were going to do even before you knew what that would be. Yes, he thought, Dr. Baden and Paul Rosenburg had been killed, and probably by the same people who were following him and watching Lester and Dale. What were they trying to keep hidden — and why did their efforts cover half of the United States?

"I know Paul Rosenburg was killed. I was supposed to meet him." David began to explain. "He was going to tell me about some weapons tests he was working on, but we never met. He was pushed over a cliff by someone before we got together."

"How horrible!" Mrs. Baden exclaimed."Yes, it was," David shuddered as he remembered the scene. "I think they are following me, now," his voice was a raspy whisper.

"My Got!" Mrs. Baden's hands covered her mouth in terror. "Vat can we do?"

"Your husband's car, do you know where it is?" David asked.

"Yes, they have taken it avay. I think it is destroyed," she answered.

"Where did they take it after the accident?" David asked.

Elsa Baden wrote an address on a card. "I know this young man. He called me to tell me they brought Karl's car to his shop. No one vould tell me anything except him."

"I'll see what I can find out," David promised, glad to at least have something to do besides worry himself.

"Thank you, David, for helping me," she told him as they prepared to part ways. "It has been difficult for me. I can trust no one else. One of those who vork vith him, maybe killed him. How can I talk to them?"

He knew she was right to be cautious. He watched her slowly walk away until her form was swallowed by the evening sunlight. David knew he could do nothing more tonight.

The shadows cast by the setting sun stretched across the green expanse of the park. The descending chill of night combined with David's apprehension to send him, shivering, to his motel.

The next morning, David contacted the mechanic who's number was on the back of Elsa's card. A young man sauntered out of the station as David drove in. David was struck by his deep Southern drawl, seemingly out of place in the desert of the American Southwest.

"Kin I hep ya, suh?" the man said as he sauntered out to meet David while wiping his greasy hands on a tattered rag.

"I'm David Seabird," David replied. "I called this morning. Are you Ron Whitney?"

"Yep, shore am," he drawled back. "Ya said somethin' 'bout lookin' at that caw we brung in couple uh days ago. They tuk it away."

David walked with the mechanic to an area behind the shop where there were a number of wrecked cars and parts scattered everywhere. They could talk freely here, David thought.

"What happened to cause Dr. Baden's accident?" David asked, as he looked intently at the young mechanic.

"I think it ain't no accident, mistuh," David struggled to translate the words that streamed from the young man. "Now, this is only my own opinion, ya see. My boss gave his statement to the police an' all. Ya' shoudda seen it round heah. Govunment types snoopin' 'round heah like crazy afta we got the caw."

"What do you mean government types?" asked David.

"Aah, ya' know, all them men in theyah dawk suits, ties, and glasses. They kinda all look like those guys in da movies, ya' know," the young man repeated.

"What did they want?" David asked with interest.

The young man answered cautiously, "They said they wanted ta know what caused the accident. My boss, he ain't none too careful sometimes, so he jist blurts it out."

"What did he blurt out?" David asked.

"Ya' know, how he never thought it ain't no accident," the young man replied.

The youth continued, "They said it must uh bin 'cause they worked with this guy an' all."

"Why were they so sure it had to be an accident?" David pressed for more.

"I dunno. I only know my boss said it looked like somebuddy'd tampud with the brakes, an' he didn't think it was no accident," Ron answered.

"What happened, then?" David asked.

"I dunno," Ron replied. "They finally left, and my boss, he said fine, musta been an accident."

"Is your boss around now?" David asked, hoping to talk to him.

"Nope," Ron said. "Went down ta Albuquerque ta the caw show. Ain't back till next week."

"What did the insurance people say about it?" David asked again.

"Dunno," Ron's reply echoed the previous few. "I don't heah much, ya know. I heard 'em talkin' 'bout suicide, but who'd cut his own brake line ta commit suicide? Don't make no sense a'tall ta me. Sounds a lot mo' like mudduh than suicide if ya ask me."

"Was there anything left in the car?" David was hopeful.

"Whata ya mean, unusual?" the young man asked in return.

"Were there any briefcases, envelopes?" David asked.

"Nope, all the personal stuff was gone before it got here," Ron answered. "My boss and me, we thought it was kinda strange. I think some bad things have happened heah, but it's my policy to keep my mouth shut, eahs open, and nose clean."

The young man smiled cautiously as he described his own philosophy. David smiled back, aware of the true danger involved in this case.

"Good policy," he said as he took out one of his business cards. David scribbled a number on the reverse and handed it to the young man. "Here's where you can reach me if you remember anything else."

"You bet, Mistuh Seabud."

David was not aware of the car which pulled out behind him at the station, and followed at a steady pace and distance as he turned down the highway to Window Rock.

Chapter 17

David had soon left the town behind, and was driving through barren land on his way to meet Joe Gaagii. The desert's beauty mesmerized David. The few trees he could see struggled to break through the sand and rocks, and had become twisted and deformed as they clawed their way to the surface. The sands were colored by reds and browns, the blinding light contrasting with deep blue shadows.

David's journey took him in and out of the canyons whose walls rose from the ground, channeling the road like a river. Fantastic sculptures carved by the wind towered over the road on both sides. Tall pinnacles topped by precariously perched boulders seemed to become figures standing beside the road, observing David's progress through the landscape.

David saw in one group of rocks what seemed to become two sailors and a dog seated above the rim of the canyon. Another became a mouse, standing on its hind legs as it stretched to reach the cheese above. One fantastic outcropping took on the profile of a haggard, old witch, complete with her tall pointed hat. Her face dissolved as he rounded the bend, only to see another figure appear in the canyon walls. The cliffs seemed to be alive, to bestow a living personality and spirit on the land.

David recalled reading how the Navajos considered this area to be the center of the earth. According to some of the mythology he had read, and these thin spires represented the forms of the ancient ancestral spirits who kept watch over the land. Thus, it was indeed, a living landscape with each element having its own personality.

The caves David could see part way up the canyon walls opened their gaping mouths. Sunlight could not penetrate into the darkness beyond, shrouding these doorways into the center of the earth in mystery. Like the eerie spire-like figures towering over the roadside, David recalled the significance of these caves in the folklore of peoples of the Southwest. The caves were where the first people emerged when they left the earth's womb to live on its sun-flooded surface.

Window Rock, from which the town took its name, came into David's view. It arched in a great expanse from one point to another, creating the large gaping opening beneath. David was amazed by this dry, barren land with its colorful decorations of fantastic rock formations. The red of the rocks contrasted with the deep blue of the sky and green of the few trees that poked their twisted heads above the white sands.

He could see why these formations had so much significance and potency for the Indians. What many would have considered dry wasteland, they revered as sacred. They sensed the aliveness of the land, recognized the personalities of its collective elements, and treated it with a healthy sense of awe. It seemed to David not just a simple sense of respect, but an awareness of the power nature could exert over its human residents, a power which could destroy as well as create.

David felt a change in atmosphere as he drove into the town, tended and tamed, separated from the earth by blocks of concrete and asphalt. He turned down a street toward the address he had been given and found himself once again on the outskirts of the city. He found Joe Gaagii's house, and was soon introducing himself.

Joe's long black hair was held in place by a blue bandanna rolled into a headband. His dark red shirt shimmered against his bronzed skin. Joe was tall and slender. David guessed he was about his own age. Joe greeted David with a solemn handshake.

"You know my 'anaalani brothers, eh?" Joe asked, smileless, as he shook David's hand.

"What kind of brothers are those?" David asked in turn, not quite understanding Joe's accent or the unfamiliar term.

"Sioux. Our way of callin' them." Joe responded.

"You mean Lester and Dale? Yeah, I know them, but haven't for long. They send their greetings," David passed on the message from the mutual friends from the north.

"How do you know them?" David was curious as he thought about the differences in geography and culture which made a chance meeting between the men seem unlikely.

"Met 'em at an Indian youth conference, years ago. Since then, I've seen 'em every year at least. Worked with Lester on land and water issues," Joe explained.

"You're a lawyer, too?" David now sensed how small the Native American community could be as he realized the common history and political interests of different tribes. "Yep," Joe said slowly. "It's a way to be an activist without getting shot."

David chuckled at the wry wit. Joe had made the statement in the same drole voice and serious expression that he had maintained since their first handshake. Only after David began to laugh did Joe smile broadly, confirming David's impression that Joe had a subtle and ironic sense of humor.

"Where did you go to school?" David asked.

Joe answered, "University of New Mexico. How about you?"

"UCLA," David said. "Journalism major." David became very serious, then continued, "I guess it's a way you can write about activists without getting shot."

Joe laughed, and David sensed he had been accepted. The little exchange helped each man to assess the other's strengths and personality before turning to the more serious business of David's mission.

"What 'id Lester send you down for?" Joe asked.

"I'm supposed to bring back something for an old man on the reservation up there. Lester said you might help me out. He also said you might be able to help me on a story I'm working on. He's involved in it," David added.

"If Lester's in it, it'll be worth workin' on," Joe answered. "What's the package you're supposed to get?"

"I don't know," David answered, "but here's the name and number I'm supposed to call about it."

David handed a note to Joe who read it, and looked up with a broad smile.

"Old Charlie Diyiini. I should'a guessed. Must be for Old Sam, eh?" Joe asked.

"Yes, you know him?" David asked in return.

"Met'im once, when I was up seein' Lester," Joe said.

"Is that Charlie's number," David asked, pointing to the paper in Joe's hand.

"No, my cousin's. Charlie doesn't have a phone," Joe answered. "Lester must'a remembered my cousin, Rex Lee, who lives up close to Charlie. He's usually the one I talk to when I need to reach Charlie."

"I guess Charlie must be like Sam, not too interested in new fangled equipment?" David said.

"Charlie's out there near Canyon de Chelly. Doesn't come into town much. He never wanted a phone in his hogan, but I don't think he could'ave had one out there anyway." Joe continued to explain Charlie's living conditions to David. "Charlie's a traditional medicine man."

"I guess he is like Sam in more ways than one," David said. "I like Sam and look forward to seeing him again."

David looked at the ground and thoughtfully drew patterns in the dirt with the toe of his shoe. He glanced back to Joe and added, "I'm looking forward to meeting Charlie."

Joe invited David into the house as he said, "We can call Rex from here and he can go down to Charlie's and make arrangements for us."

After making the call to Rex, the two men went for lunch at a cafe nearby. They returned to the house where they waited for Rex's call to advise them of word from Charlie. A short time later, they were on the road from Window Rock to Canyon de Chelly.

"You said you'd been talkin' to Lester 'bout a story. How can I help out?" Joe brought up the remark from their initial conversation.

"I was sent to South Dakota to investigate a story about the crash of a rocket or satellite. Some kind of weapons test that went awry. A tip came in from a high-level government insider." David began to recount the events leading to his meeting Joe and their trip to see Charlie.

"I was supposed to meet this man at a pre-arranged point, at Mt. Rushmore actually, but he was killed before I could talk to him. Now I find out that another man down here who was working with him on the project was also killed. It was supposed to look like an accident or suicide, but it was clearly murder." David explained.

"How does this fit with meeting Lester and Dale?" Joe asked.

"I met them on something different. Actually, I met Dale in a bar the first night I was in Rapid City," David said.

"Sounds about right," Joe chuckled.

"Seems he knew Sam Going Away. I had read about Sam before I left LA, and Dale volunteered to take me out to see him."

"What was the interest in Sam?" Joe asked.

"Partly just curiosity. I've always been interested in Indian issues. And my boss thought it might help as a cover story for my real research up there," David answered.

"How does Sam fit into this?" Joe pressed for more information, sounding like the young lawyer he was.

"I read this press release about him taking in some stranger — there's a dispute over who has jurisdiction in Indian Country. I was going to follow up on why the authorities wanted this stranger, why Sam took him in, where he came from, all of that," David said.

"So what'd ya find out?" Joe asked.

"Not much. Met Lester. He and Dale took me out to meet Sam. But something strange happened," David said.

"Oh yeah?" Joe asked. "What?"

"I don't really know how to explain it," David started to explain. "Sam wouldn't let me meet the stranger. Said I would when it was time. But it seems that Lester and Dale are aware of the weapons testing facility. They say some of them on the Reservation have actually been able to infiltrate the plant."

"Holy..." Joe started to mutter.

"Yeah," agreed David. "We went out to see the crash site."

"What'd ya find?" Joe asked.

"We didn't find anything then," David said. "Lester and Dale said their people had found something right after the crash. When we got there, someone found us."

Joe glanced over at David, speechless.

"Yeah, we were followed. Helicopters, cars. In fact, I've been followed since I left LA. Seems like someone knows me better than I know myself. They know where I'm going before I do."

"Scared?" Joe asked.

"What do you think?" David asked ironically.

"Are we being followed now?" Joe looked out the window and behind the car as if expecting to see something or someone in view.

"I suspect we are, but I don't know for sure. They knew I was coming to Gallup." David could feel the fear constricting his neck and beginning to choke. He had to think about something else, if only to survive. Instead of changing the subject, though, he said, "It appears all of this is somehow connected to Lester's investigation of the military installation up there. Lester said you had been looking into some similar situations down here, some mysterious things going on. I think someone wants secrets to stay secret."

Joe said, "I think you're right there. There's more to my work with Lester than land and water rights."

It was David's turn to glance in surprise at Joe. Joe continued, "We've been workin' together on several 'unofficial' military installations near Indian lands. The military, they deny these bases exist, so they sure aren't gonna admit anything 'bout what they're doin' there."

"Good point," David agreed.

Joe continued, "Lester has some of the information about the testing they're doin' in the ionosphere."

"I know. He told me a little about it," David said.

"You know this is not just an Indian problem. It could have a devastatin' impact on the whole earth. Does your weapons problem fit into this?"

"I think so," David said. "I'm not sure how, but I think it's all connected. Lester said something about UFO activity up there about the time the thing came down. He thinks some strange things are involved in all this business."

"We've talked some about it. Ya know, there've been unexplained things goin' on down here for years now."

"I remember this being a hot spot for UFO sightings," David said. "Wasn't it down here somewhere that one supposedly crashed forty or fifty years ago?"

"You must be talkin' 'bout Roswell," Joe said. "The whole incident's been back in the news recently. Someone supposedly filmed an autopsy on one of the alien bodies from the crash."

"What do you think it was," David probed.

"I dunno what to think," Joe's response was careful, and he thought as he spoke slowly. "There are those who think the whole thing was a hoax and the body was a fake. Some think it was a real alien and the government didn't want anyone to know at the time because it would cause panic. Now they don't want to admit they lied. Others think the government was conducting its own experiments, maybe running tests on their own citizens."

"Wouldn't that be too obvious?" David asked.

"Not if they were doing tests on people no one knew were alive," Joe answered.

"You mean 'undesirables'?" David winced as he thought about the meaning of the word. The full horror of the implications of this scenario was beginning to dawn on him.

"Yes, someone 'they' didn't think had a right to live. Someone from an institution, maybe, or someone with a strange disease taken at birth," Joe said, the disgust evident in his voice.

"How would a parent allow such a thing," David asked.

"Maybe they never knew. They might have been told their baby died, when it hadn't," Joe answered.

"It sounds so horrible," David said, "like playing God."

"You wouldn't expect the government to brag about something like that, would you?" Joe asked sarcastically.

"No, and it would explain why the questions still don't get answered after all this time," David agreed.

"We've wondered about those UFO sightings out here, too," Joe continued. "They could be related to atmospheric research or weapons testing, or maybe they are from outer space. The military is still not telling us everything."

"Have there been any sightings recently?" David asked.

"Yeah, quite a few. I don't know if they call it 'flap' or not, but we've had some." Joe paused in thought, then added a new topic to the conversation. "You heard about cattle mutilations around here?"

"Tell me about them," David said."Some people don't think there's any connection between mutilations and UFO's, but it sure seems like UFO's are seen about the same times and places that we find mutilated cattle or other animals," Joe explained.

"Any particular kind of animal involved?" David asked.

"They've found cattle, sheep, horses. Even dogs have died, but I don't know if anything happened to them. The first one, I guess, was a pony." Joe paused in thought and they drove on in silence for a few moments.

"What happens?" David asked.

"The animals are found lying in a field somewhere. Lots of times, there aren't any hoof prints or footprints or anything around the carcasses. It's like they were picked up where they stood, then were dropped back into the field after whoever took them was done with them," Joe said.

"Strange," David said.

"Most of them look like different parts of their bodies have been cut or burned," Joe continued. "There's usually no blood, like its been drained out of 'em."

"How do they know a predator hasn't killed the animals?" David asked.

"Maybe they did, but the cuts don't look like animal bites. You know any predator who burns a hole in its victim?" Joe asked. "Can you explain how one animal can kill another and not leave any blood on the ground?"

"Who would do that to animals?" David asked, thinking of his own pets and how hurt he would feel if something happened to them.

"If someone would experiment with human beings, they wouldn't think anything about tests on animals," Joe answered.

"How horrible," David said quietly.

"I agree. You see what we could be up against?" Joe pointed out the seriousness of their position.

They drove on in silence, each lost in thought.

"What do you think?" David finally broke the silence.

"It's like the UFO's. I dunno what to think. It might be the government testing something, but I don't know what. They could pick animals up with some kind of aircraft, take what they need, or do whatever they do, then dump the carcass back on the ground. Maybe big business is involved."

"What would they have to do with it," David wondered out loud.

"Accordin' to those who think this, the whole thing is a high tech cattle rustlin' racket. Somethin' like pharmaceutical companies tryin' to get supplies for exotic and expensive drugs," Joe answered.

"Doesn't that seem a little farfetched?" David asked.

"Maybe. Maybe not," Joe said. "You know what people can be like when money is involved. Some people think big business is in with the government in some kind of conspiracy."

"I guess I can see how such a cooperation could be beneficial to both business and government," David said. "There must be some other explanation."

Joe provided another theory. "There are some who think aliens are responsible."

"For the mutilations? Why?" David asked.

"Some people 'round here say it would explain why UFO's and mutilations seem to occur at the same time," Joe explained. "They think the aliens might be conductin' experiments on animals. Maybe they are curious, or maybe they need something from the parts they're takin'. If they need somethin' to survive, maybe they're out lookin' for it. Or findin' it on earth."

"What do you think it is?" David asked Joe.

"I know there's some strange things out here," Joe said. "I've seen a few weird things in my life I don't know how to explain, and I know other people who could say the same. I dunno what to think, but my mind's open."

They drove on in silence, and David thought about Joe's words. Science could not provide all the answers. Any of the explanations could be right, but none of them were comforting. Government conspiracies or covers would not be beneficial whether they resulted from deliberate actions against citizens or from more noble, but fruitless, attempts to shield them from the truth. If the explanation came from another world ... David could not imagine what it might involve.

The passing scenery raced past David's fixed gaze. The world around him finally pushed his fear and concerns from the forefront of his mind. Pinion pines and juniper trees dotted the golden landscape, making splashes of green against the rocky hills. Their twisted and gnarled trunks related the struggle for survival in this harsh environment.

Greenish gray sage brush, with blossoms of gold scented the air. The perfume triggered memories that flooded David's consciousness. He felt himself riding in the family car, a child again. The scent of the sage brush made him remember the trip, years before. He recalled the warmth of safety within his parent's care, the excitement of a new adventure on their Rocky Mountain holiday.

He realized with sadness the loss of security that he felt. This trip might be an adventure, but it was not one filled with fun. It was fraught with danger and uncertainty.

Joe directed David to turn off the highway and onto a dirt road. The car which had tailed David from the time he and Joe left town, followed at a discreet distance.

Chapter 18

When Joe and David left the main highway to follow a dirt road leading into a canyon, the driver of the car tailing them missed the event. David and Joe had crossed the railroad tracks before the long freight train blocked traffic on the highway. The second car had not been so fortunate. Its driver, therefore, sped past the turnoff and on down the highway.

David drove down the canyon road for about four miles. He decided the canyon walls must have soared at least six hundred feet above them and the small river that snaked between the road and the cliffs.

"You see the gully up there?" Joe broke the silence as he leaned forward and pointed between two walls through which a stream flowed to join the river. "Up there on the top is where my cousin, Rex, has his winter hogan. We called him to get in touch with Charlie."

"What's a winter hogan?" David asked. "Does he have more than one?"

"Rex has three," Joe started to explain. "It's necessary for us. The hogan is a home for our people."

Joe paused and David waited, trying to be patient until Joe continued his explanation.

"Most people don't have three homes, eh?" Joe asked, a smile lighting up his face. "We don't have them because we're rich, though. We hafta keep movin' all through the year."

"Why must you move so often?" David asked.

"We hafta move the sheep so they'll have enough to eat, and good places to have their lambs," Joe said.

"Why is the rim of the canyon better in the winter?" David asked again.

"There's trees and grasses up there," Joe said. "We can feed them up there. It's easier to get to town, too."

"Do you move in the spring?" David asked, vaguely aware of the sound of the river and of birds singing in the trees lining its banks.

"It warms up here in the canyon," Joe explained. "There's still snow up there sometimes. We bring them down here and shear the sheep. Then we stay here for a while and move to the summer hogan."

"I've seen the famous Navajo rugs," David said. "They are beautiful."

Joe beamed with pride as he described the process of creating these works of art.

"We shear the sheep and clean the wool," Joe said. "Our women take the wool and card it and spin it into threads. When I was young, I used to help gather the plants my grandmother used to dye the wool into the right colors."

David was curious. "How do you know which plants to use?"

"I dunno," Joe answered. "The old folks just know and teach the younger ones the right way. We used to help put skeins of wool into the pots to dye them, and my mother and grandmother would hang them in the trees to dry."

"Are there special patterns to follow when they weave the rugs?" David asked.

"Sorta," Joe said. "My grandmother was good at making a design as she worked on the loom. Some weavers aren't as good at it."

Joe paused before continuing to tell David how the weaving was done. "The women string up a loom and use a beater to hammer down the strands they weave. I remember falling asleep to the sound of my mother and grandmother weaving."

"How does it sound," David asked.

"It's just a thumping sound. Like a drum from a far away place," Joe said dreamily.

"This place reminds me of when I was a kid, too," David said. "You mind if we stop for a minute? It smells so good here, like spring."

"Smells make you remember things when your eyes and ears don't, eh?" Joe observed.

David pulled to the edge of the road and stopped the car. The two men emerged into the sunshine streaming into the canyon. The gurgling of the stream added to the chorus of birds in the rustling trees along the riverbank. David was overwhelmed with contentment and a sense of well-being for the first time in many days, it seemed. He sniffed the air, recalling summer swimming trips with his uncles and cousins in a willow-lined creek much like this one. He had forgotten those childhood memories, and it was good to have them return to his consciousness.

David became aware of another sound in addition to the music of the birds, breeze, and brook. It was a man chanting in the distance.

"Do you hear singing?" David asked Joe.

"Sounds like Charlie," Joe said. "Must be payin' his respects to Mother Earth."

David strained to listen to the chanting. He was enchanted by the beauty of the place, the warmth of the sun, the smells and sounds that engulfed him. He was warm and safe, protected as if in the womb of the earth. Joe broke his reverie.

"Charlie's place is close. He expects us," Joe said with such confidence David wondered if Joe had some secret way of knowing other men's thoughts. The place was so peaceful and serene David almost resented the necessity of continuing the journey, but he knew other experiences awaited him.

David drove around a bend and into the area occupied by Charlie's hogan and pens. The small circular hut with a conical roof was surrounded by cottonwood and willow trees. The nearby pens kept sheep and horses. Other sheep grazed in a flat grassy area near the river.

A couple of dogs lazily lounged in the shade of a weeping willow, and David spotted two more beneath a wagon near the door of the hogan. The dogs beneath the tree ignored the two new arrivals, while those beneath the wagon yawned and stretched without much concern or ambition. One rose and strolled over to greet the visitors as they walked toward the hogan's owner.

The entire family was working outside the hogan. Charlie was seated before a small fire near a tiny structure David thought might be a sweat lodge. Charlie was singing to the small child he was bouncing on his knee. The child began to laugh and Charlie, himself, broke into peals of laughter. A young girl stood behind Charlie's shoulder and played with the baby, too. Other children were playing on a swing made of an old tire suspended from the branch of a cottonwood tree. Beneath the nearby willow, two women sat weaving at large, vertical looms. The scene was one of domestic simplicity and tranquillity. David was sorry to disturb the picture by their arrival.

One of the dogs walked beside them, its tail wagging slightly. The rest looked up and decided not to venture into the sun. The children were more enthusiastic. Those at the swing left their play and came shouting their greeting to Joe.

"Uncle" Joe picked up one the younger children and tossed him into the air, catching him as he fell back from the sky. Then he gave another a big hug. Joe greeted each of the children individually.

David followed the parade as dog, children and Joe moved toward where Charlie sat waiting for them.

"Welcome," Charlie greeted the two men in his raspy, heavily accented, but soft voice. "I knew you would come," he said as David was introduced to him.

Charlie was tall and fit. His graying hair was tied into a knot held by a piece of blue cloth. His weathered face, lined like the canyon walls around him, did not detract from his vigorous and strong appearance, but gave him an air of serenity, peace, and wisdom.

Charlie's wife, Rachel, beamed with pride at the large, playful brood surrounding her. They brought joy to her hogan, the home where the Navajo ate, slept, and lived together.

She invited Joe and David to eat fry bread and drink tea. Joe visited with Rachel and Charlie over tea, as David watched the girls prepare to bake bread for use later. David could not understand what Joe and Charlie were saying, but the rhythm of the language was like a lullaby to him. The tea, the warmth of the day, and the quiet, lilting words passing between the visiting friends made him drowsy and content.

Joe soon nudged him, conveying Charlie's invitation to join him in a sweat. Charlie prepared the fire to heat the rocks used inside the lodge. He used a shovel to take the hot rocks inside the tiny lodge, and closed the opening with a skin. Throughout the preparation of the lodge, Charlie also prepared himself. He turned to each of the four directions of the wind and sang a song. David looked at Joe who answered his unspoken question.

"He is calling the Holy Ones to join him here," Joe said.

When the preparations were complete, the three men entered the sweat lodge. Near the end of their time in the sweat, Charlie spoke in English to David, but David did not know what it meant.

"You were sent by my friend, Sam. I know now your heart is good. You must return a gift to Sam for me." Charlie said nothing more, but led them outside where he lay on the ground and spread dirt over his body.

"You dry yourself with Mother Earth," Joe explained, following Charlie's example.

David did the same, recalling how he used to watch horses roll in the dirt to dry themselves once they were freed from bridles and saddles. He caught himself thinking he must be dirtier than when he started his bath, but was aware of both physical and spiritual rejuvenation and cleansing.

The sky had undergone a transformation while they were in the sweatlodge. To the west, the sun struggled to shine from behind the dark, threatening clouds. A great, towering thunderhead boiled high above the earth, as the wind picked up below.

Even the moods of the animals had changed. The dogs were no longer sleeping beneath the trees. The ponies kicked up their heels, running from one end of the pen to the other in agitation. The sheep and goats flowed like a great white whirlpool, following one another in a crowded circle around the pen. David, too, could feel the electricity in the air, the anticipation of the coming storm.

Then all seemed still. The birds had Red to their shelter, the dogs sniffed the air, as if to follow the storm's progress. It broke with a fury, shattering the stillness. Great drops of rain poured from the sky, blown against the side of the hogan by the wind which seemed to have increased its rage after the brief moments of calm before the storm.

The canyon was illuminated by the white flashes of lightning. It's walls echoed and rebounded, the thunder crashing through the seething clouds. David had never before seen such a storm. He sat with Joe and the children against the side of the hogan, protected by its walls from the wind, both excited and terrified by this awesome display of nature's raw and unbridled power.

Charlie, his eyes closed in meditation, also sat with them. He calmly opened his large black eyes and spoke to David in English. "Our Mother is pleased with your cleansing sweat, and cleans herself with the rain."

The fury of the storm was spent within twenty minutes. The rain, which caused rivulets to run down the road, stopped as quickly as it had begun. The sun reappeared through the clouds and painted a bright rainbow in the sky above the canyon walls. David became aware of the birds starting to chirp in the rain-drenched branches of the willows and cottonwoods. The feelings of expectancy and anticipation were replaced by those of fulfillment and completion.

David was exhausted by the day's events and emotions. He could have skipped supper and gone to bed if he had been in his own home, but instead, he joined the family and felt refreshed by the food.

It was good he had been revived, for the day was far from over. After supper, a sick neighbor was brought to Charlie, who was to perform a healing ceremony. David, cleansed and prepared by Charlie, was invited to participate in the event.

The sick man was laid on a rug in a corner of the ceremony hut. David watched as Charlie took buckets of different colors of sand and spread out an earth-colored canvas for a sand painting.

Joe had explained to David how Navajo sand paintings could be of two different types, public art or secret ceremonial paintings. Joe said Charlie spent many of his waking hours gathering the minerals for his palette from different places in the Navajo lands.

"The canyon walls have veins of different kinds and colors of minerals. Somebody who is gonna make sand-paintings begins his apprenticeship with the elders or spiritual people when he is young," Joe had said.

David thought Charlie must have been creating sand paintings for many years. Joe had explained how practice could change perception for the artists.

"They have a different way of lookin' at the canyon walls. They can see the different colors trapped in them, and they free the colors," Joe said.

Charlie had prepared the sands by grinding the chunks of minerals between rocks to make a fine sand. Each color was stored in its own bucket. David was amazed at the variety and intensity of the colors. He had not seen the deep lazuli blues and vibrant greens in the sandy canyon walls as they had driven through them. He had been aware only of the reds and yellows of the sandstone. Charlie had pinks and reds, greens and blues, yellows and browns, white and black, all carefully chosen and stored.

Charlie spread out the dark earth-colored sand into an even square about two inches deep. He chanted as he began to create figures and geometric patterns by letting the sand sift through an opening in his fingers.

David watched in fascination as the images took their forms within the geometric boundaries of the sand-painting. First Charlie painted the backgrounds, dividing the square into four quadrants, each a different color.

Joe explained quietly to David, "Each of the colors represents a time and a direction. The white is for the mornin' and the east with its risin' sun. The blue is for the middle of the day and the direction of south. The yellow is for the west and the settin' sun of evening. The black is the northern star and for night."

Once the quadrants were painted their appropriate colors, Charlie drew more figures and symbols over the background. Joe explained, "Charlie is makin' an image to restore balance. This is necessary to heal the sick man."

When Charlie was finished, the sick man was made to sit upon the painting. This, Joe explained, was done to convey the universal balance of the painting into the sick man and accomplish its healing purpose.

David thought of Holly and wished she could see this. She would be envious of experiences all through this day.

He became aware of the ending of the ceremony, and returned his attention to it.

"Charlie is about to put away the painting," Joe said. David was about to ask what this meant when Joe continued the explanation. "This has to be done in a symbolic way. He must move from east to south to west to north."

David was still puzzled, until he watched Charlie "put the painting away." Charlie reached across the painting and drew the sand towards the center. Next, he pulled the sand from the right, swept up the sand from the bottom of the painting, and finally from the left. All the colored sands were buried within the mound of earth-colored soil.

David thought it was a pity to destroy such a beautiful work of art, but Joe explained the reason.

"To you, this might seem like destruction," Joe whispered, "but to us, it is regeneration. The energy of the painting is given back to the earth."

It was like the afternoon storm. What seemed violent and destructive was life-giving, regenerative. The energy of the storm, like the painting's positive energy, restored the balance of the earth.

The rest of the evening was a magical education for David. He sat with Rachel as she worked on a rug. She explained the meanings of the various patterns on the rugs, taught to her by her mother and grandmother. She, like them, passed this knowledge on to her children.

Without patterns or pictures to follow, the designs for her rugs would develop, Rachel explained. She could anticipate when and where the colors needed to be changed to make the patterns emerge.

Rachel wove each strand among the framework of threads strung onto the loom. She used her "beater," a tool looking to David like something between a stick and a comb, to force the yarn tightly against the last layer of yarn. This caused the thumping sound Joe had recalled with such fondness.

Rachel had a fine rhythm to her work. Although she visited with Joe, her hands never slowed down, but flashed among the vertical threads as she wove the yarn among them, followed by the thudding sound of the beater against the yarn. The rhythm of Rachel's weaving was like all those of traditional Navajo life. The seasons, the days, and the moments all seemed to David to be metrical, continuous, and unchanging.

Joe had told David the Navajo system was matriarchal. Rachel had inherited this property from her mother, and it would be passed on to one of her daughters.

David watched the children as they were entertained by Charlie's songs and stories. The sense of family seemed so strong here, but the individual people also showed character and fortitude. Maybe the strength of the family was tied to the reverence for and dependence upon the land. Almost everything this family had was a gift of the land. Without the plants and animals the land provided, the family had nothing. With them, they were rich.

David was conscious of the flickering lamplight and the metrical thud of Rachel's beater weaving life into the strands of wool on her loom. It was a drumbeat that echoed the rhythm of his own heart. As he drifted to sleep, it seemed to increase in volume, thundering through his restless dreams. He saw himself running from the helicopters, their blades thumping out the steady rhythm. He ran into canyons without exits and fell from cliffs, endlessly tumbling through space, but never able to escape his pursuers.

Chapter 19

The next morning, David was awakened by an unfamiliar hammering sound. He roused himself, and stood at the door of the hogan watching Charlie and Rachel beating together cobs of dried corn. The kernels dropped from the ears into buckets placed before them.

They greeted him, and invited David to join them. Charlie talked while he continued to shuck the ears of corn. His voice was soft and rhythmic.

"This is a sacred plant for us Navajos," Charlie said. "The corn was given to our ancestors by visitors from another world. It is our most important gift."

David listened, sipping coffee, and gazing at the hawks soaring between the canyon walls. They were effortlessly hitching a ride on the currents of air warmed by the morning sun.

Joe appeared at the door with fresh coffee. The two men helped Charlie and Rachel finish their work. When the corn was put away, Charlie took Joe and David past the sheep pen, pointed down the road beyond, and reminded David why he had come.

"It is time for your work," Charlie said. "Go there to the caves of the ancestors. You will be given a gift to bring back to Sam."

Charlie turned and walked back to his hogan, the dogs following behind him. Joe and David stood watching Charlie walk away, then proceeded down the road beside the river.

David had no idea what Charlie was talking about, but it seemed pointless to try and ask the old man who was already diminishing into the distance.

"Do you know what he is talking about," David sought Joe's opinion.

"Nope. But when he says to do somethin', you should do it. I'll take you up to the caves," Joe volunteered.

The cliffs beside them darted in and out of the bright sunshine. David was aware of the sweet smell of the plants growing along the bank. A cool breeze gently rustled the leaves of the cottonwood trees.

Joe pulled him aside and they began to climb up a ridge. At the top, they looked across a broad gully.

"There's somethin' here you should see," he told David.

"Where?" David asked.

"Down there. In those caves," Joe answered.

"What's there?" David squinted against the sun to make out the black holes nearly obscured by the pinion trees which covered their entrances.

"Fine art," Joe answered.

They scrambled over rocks and scrub brush to see petroglyphs etched into the rock beneath the overhang of a cliff. David gasped in surprise. There before him was the same figure he had seen with Holly at the art gallery. It had the long arms and thin, wavy legs; the neck was stretched above the body, and supporting a head formed of concentric circles, from which lines radiated like sun rays.

Other figures and geometric drawings covered the canyon wall. Some were zig-zags, others were curvilinear patterns.

"These write a story about the history of our people," Joe said.

"What does the story tell?" David asked, interested in the meaning of the designs.

"They tell how corn was brought to our people," Joe said.

"Who brought the corn?" David asked, trying to work out the story in pictures.

"Gods from another world," Joe answered.

Joe pointed to one particular group of scratches on the rock face. The main petroglyph showed an oval object with lines streaming from its base.

"It shows here the way they came to us," Joe explained.

"If I didn't know better, I'd say it looks like a drawing of a UFO," David observed.

"Yeah," Joe agreed.

"Why did it come here? Does it say?" David inquired.

"Something happened to their craft," Joe explained. "It flew like a bird in the sky, but something went wrong with it. They had to fix it."

Joe pointed to a series of zig-zag marks on the rock.

"See these?" he asked David. "They show how they fixed their ship."

"How did they do it?" David asked in return.

"I don't know all this story," Joe replied. "I only remember some of the old people said it was a picture of energy."

"Of energy," David repeated. "Yeah, I think I see it. They do look like the pictures you see of light waves or radio waves or something."

"The old people say it shows history, science, everything important for our people to know," Joe said. "They say it's sacred writing, because religion is remembering all of this. Sacred ceremonies of people on earth help them remember the past, and preserve knowledge of how to live in this world. It gives meaning to our lives."

David gazed at the drawings as he thought about the truth of Joe's words. Even the religious celebrations of Western European cultures, like Christianity, were remembrances and reenactments of the history of a Visitor from another world who came to earth to bring new meaning to human existence. He thought he would have a new attitude about Christmas from now on.

Joe led David down a rough path until they reached the mouth of one of the caves they had seen from the canyon rim. As they entered, David became aware of the oppressive heat and darkness within the cave.

"Don't we need a light?" David asked.

"I've been here before. I know the way," Joe answered, still leading David deeper into the darkness.

The darkness was almost more than David could bear. He stumbled on a rock and twisted his ankle. He was becoming impatient with Joe for bringing him here without so much as a light. Suddenly, he heard a strange sound, a rattle.

"Stand still," demanded Joe.

"I hurt my ankle," answered David. "I can't move easily in this dark."

"Just don't move. You hear that sound?" Joe continued.

"Yeah, is it a rattlesnake?" David asked.

"That or something pretending to be," Joe whispered as he returned to David's side. "What happened to your ankle?"

"I tripped on a rock. Why are we walking around a black cave with no light anyway?" David asked with an edge to his voice.

"Charlie sent us here," Joe said matter-of-factly. "I told you when he says to do something, you just do it."

"What are we going to do about the snake?" David asked.

"We're going to wait," Joe answered.

They did wait, it seemed for hours. David and Joe sat silently in the darkness. David could not see his watch, and could not make out how long they were sitting motionless. He was overcome with a desire to close his eyes and sleep, his head resting against the side of the cave where the two men sat side by side.

Whether he dreamed it or was awakened by it, David was not certain, but a brilliant light flooded the cavern. He could see that the walls were covered with paintings and designs that echoed those he had seen earlier that day, if indeed it was the same day. Before him stood a shining form he had seen before. It was "Seagod" from Seegook's painting. It was the same image that he had dreamed or seen standing before the window of his hotel in Rapid City. He could not think, but was overwhelmed with sensations he could not distinguish, or even fully recall when he tried to think about it later.

The shimmering form came near him. David was blinded by the light. A voice, almost disembodied, echoed from the cavern walls. "Seagoyuk," the voice called him. David froze, hearing the name he had been given years before by Old Man Koongoosuk in Alaska.

As he watched, half in fearful awe and half in excited amazement, the shimmering image transformed into the form of a man — a man David had seen before. Seegook stood before him, or was it merely an image of Seegook?

"Seegook?" David stammered.

"Yes, it's me," Seegook answered, but in a more hollow voice than David had remembered when he met him in Los Angeles.

David could not speak. He knew they were communicating. He could hear his own voice, as well as Seegook's, but he could not consciously make his mouth form the words, or his voice give life to them.

"You must take this to Sam," Seegook said as he placed a small box in David's hands.

"What is it?" David asked.

"You will learn all you need to know," Seegook answered, and with the brief exchange, he transformed once more into the shimmering "Seagod" of David's dreams. As the image faded, the cave returned to blackness and David to sleep.

David opened his eyes some time later — he could not make out how long it had been since his vivid dream, if that was what it had been.

He realized the cave was half-lit by a shaft of sunlight. It had been black before. Why was the sun able to light it now. He realized Joe was asleep beside him and he shook his unconscious form.

"What happened," Joe stammered as he wiped the sleep from his eyes.

"Didn't you see anything?" David asked in disbelief.

"No, I didn't," Joe answered. "I remember coming in here, and you saying you hurt your ankle just before we heard the rattlesnake."

David thought everything was a dream, then, except he had a small package on his lap. It had been real. And his ankle didn't hurt anymore. All of this, his hurting his ankle, the rattlesnake, must have just been a way to make them stop right here, right then.

"Let's go," David declared.

"What about the snake?" Joe asked.

"There isn't any snake," David answered with renewed confidence.

"How about your ankle? You gonna be ok?" Joe asked.

"It's fine. We have what we came here for," David said.

"What did we come here for?" Joe seemed puzzled.

"This," David said as he held up the small box.

"Where did you get it?" Joe asked, bewildered.

"Didn't you see the light? Didn't you see Seegook?" David asked.

"Who's Seegook?" Joe asked.

David realized Joe had been completely unaware of the events in the cave. If it was not for the tangible box in his hands, he would never have believed it was anything but a dream himself.

"I'll tell you on the way back," David said. "Let's get out of here."

The two men left the cave as David recounted his experience and how he had received the box. They returned to the road and shuffled along silently in the dust. There were no cars, no planes, no sounds of technology. Only the rustling of leaves and the babbling of a nearby brook broke the silence of what seemed to David a shimmering dreamscape.

David felt drowsy, yet at peace. He imagined himself walking on air, inches above the ground; floating beside Joe in a world without time. The heat of the morning was visible as it rose from the rocks to return to the heavens from which it came. It distorted David's vision, making the rocks bend and quiver, the canyon walls dislodge from their mooring to float above the men. Flashing pools of liquid before them reflected the dreamlike scene, only to disappear and sink into the dust as they approached.

He and Joe said nothing. For them, time lost all meaning. They seemed to have stepped into some parallel universe. If David had thought of it, he would have described it as walking into an abstract painting; but he was thinking of nothing. Only when Charlie's hogan came into sight did the two men walk out of their dream and back into time.

Chapter 20

Charlie sat bouncing one of the grandchildren on his knee. Rachel was kneading bread nearby. Joe and David approached, greeted by Charlie's welcoming smile.

"You have what you came here for," Charlie told David in his soft, heavy accent. "You are welcome here, but you must return with the gift to Sam."

David sensed an urgency to begin his trip back to South Dakota. He knew he hadn't finished his work here, but he felt compelled to take the box to Sam before doing anything else.

He and Joe bid their farewells to Charlie and Rachel, and began the long drive to town. David looked at his watch, absently gauging how long the trip would take. With surprise, he found it had stopped sometime during their adventure in the cave. It seemed to be running fine now, but there were several hours missing, at least if the clock in the car was correct.

"Do you have the time?" David asked Joe.

"Two o'clock," Joe answered, looking at the watch on his wrist.

"My watch says the same," David said, puzzled. "The clock in the car says it's five already."

David switched on the radio, and the news at the top of the hour confirmed the later time.

"Why did both our watches stop for the same length of time, I wonder?" David said, almost thinking out loud.

"I've heard of this happenin', but it never happened to me before," Joe said slowly.

"What happening?" David asked.

"Losin' time. Maybe we were somewhere else for a few hours without remembering it," Joe said.

"Did you feel strange when we were walking back from the cave?" David asked, seeking some explanation for his own weird experience.

"Like I was dreamin'," Joe answered. "You felt it, too?" he asked.

"I thought I was walking, but not on the ground," David said. "You were there, but you seemed far away somehow. I didn't feel like talking."

"Nothin' seemed real to me, but I thought I was havin' a hallucination or somethin'," Joe added. "I didn't know it was happenin' to you, too."

David felt comforted by the fact his experience had been shared, but puzzled and disturbed by what had happened. He, in fact, was not certain just what they had been through.

David turned off the radio and they drove in silence, absorbed by their thoughts of the day. The setting sun painted the sky behind them in an array of brilliant reds and oranges. By the time they stopped at a roadside cafe for supper, the colors had faded into deep blue and the stars were beginning to appear.

As they returned to the car, David could hear the rhythmic thudding of the helicopter. He searched the area of the sky where the sound originated. Two pinpoints of light marked the craft, which hovered menacingly, its dark mass blocking out the light of the stars behind it. David shivered, realizing it was probably following them at a discreet distance. Out of the corner of his eye, a flickering light illuminated the face of a man in a dark car parked near them, and went out after he lit his cigarette. David thought nothing of it until the car pulled out after them and followed them down the road into the desert night.

Neither man said much as they drove the dark, deserted highway. The desert which had seemed so beautiful and colorful to David in the daylight, now was filled with sinister shadows and forms. The towering rocks which lined the road stood like somber hooded monks on their way to a ghostly mass in the ruins of a deserted abbey.

"It's spooky out here at night, isn't it?" David said at last.

"Can be," Joe agreed. "I wouldn't want to be lost out here at night."

"Me neither," David concurred. "At least, we aren't alone. A car has been behind us since we left the cafe." The thought of it did not make David happy, the nervous edge to his voice betraying his fear and the irony of the remark.

The driver of the dark car increased its speed, decreasing the distance between him and David. After following closely for a mile or two, the car behind sounded a siren, and flashing lights lit up the black landscape.

"Guess we would have been better off alone," David mumbled as he looked for a wide place to pull off the road.

The dark, unmarked car slowed behind him and came to a stop. David watched two men emerge from the car and begin to walk toward his. As the light fell on their faces, David gasped, and without warning to Joe, put the car in gear. The tires squealed as David stepped on the gas and sped down the highway. He could see the two men race back to their car to begin their pursuit.

"What do ya think you're doin'?" Joe yelled. "We're in trouble now."

"They aren't cops," David said. His palms were wet and slippery against the steering wheel. "They were in South Dakota where the man I was supposed to meet was killed. They were pretending to be security agents at the airport."

"You're gettin' paranoid," Joe declared, "but I guess it's better than bein' dead. You think we can outrun them?"

"We'll have to try," David said. "I don't think anyone would find us out here anytime soon if they catch up with us."

David drove as fast as he ever had, but he was not used to this kind of thing. Joe braced himself, and shut his eyes in terror more than once.

David's efforts were to no avail. The car chasing them gradually decreased the distance and soon was close behind. The driver pulled the dark car into the lane beside David, just as Joe shouted a warning to him.

"Watch out, he's got a gun!" Joe could see the gun pushed through the passenger window, aimed at David.

David slammed on his brakes, successfully avoiding the shot he and Joe could almost see explode from the gun. The lights of an oncoming car appeared over the hill, and tires squealed as all three cars swerved and narrowly missed colliding.

The dark car with the two men rammed David's car with a thump, and David had to struggle for control.

"They're gonna kill us!" Joe yelled.

David yelled back, "Get down! We don't want to give them another target!"

David, with one eye on the dark road ahead of him and the other on the rear-view mirror, was aware that the desert in front of him was being lit up by spotlights. The helicopter which had followed them was almost over the dark car behind them.

There was nothing David could do. If the men in the car did not kill them, the men in the helicopter would. It was only a matter of how and when they were going to die. Well, he wasn't going to go out without a fight, and he knew Joe wouldn't either. He stomped on the accelerator, urging the car on.

"What's that?" Joe yelled as he pointed ahead of them. Three lights, moving faster than anything they had seen before were swooping down in front the car. In a bright flash, they flew over David's car.

"Wow!" David exclaimed, following the track of the lights in the rear view mirror.

An explosion rocked the car, nearly causing David to lose control.

"What's that?" Joe turned quickly to see the helicopter engulfed in flames. The bright orange and yellow of the fire fell onto the dark car behind them. It tumbled off the road and into a ravine where it, too, exploded into flames.

"Stop," Joe demanded.

"Are you crazy?" David answered.

"No, there's nobody to follow us now," Joe declared.

David pulled to the side of the road and both men emerged to witness the carnage behind them. The wreckage of the helicopter was strewn on and along the highway; the car burned where it had come to a stop after being thrown from the road. Only the roar of the flames broke the silence.

As they watched, a bright light appeared on the horizon. In paralyzed silence, they watched as it came closer without a sound. It was a great, fiery diamond revolving in the sky, streams of light emerging from it to light up patches of desert landscape. It hovered over the mangled helicopter. An intense beam shot out from beneath the unfamiliar craft, blinding David and Joe. They averted their eyes for only a moment, but during that brief period, the desert returned to darkness. The two men opened their eyes to find nothing in the road — no flames, no wreckage, no bodies, no hovering craft. Nothing but a quiet desert road. The great craft had swept it clean and disappeared into the heavens.

David and Joe stared at each other in voiceless disbelief. They silently returned to their car and resumed their journey.

"What do you think they wanted?" Joe asked.

"Who? The people in the car, or in that other thing, whatever it is?" David asked. "You know, I think that other thing was protecting us. They weren't after us at all. They were after them"

"I'm confused," Joe said. "Them, us ..."

"I think the men in the helicopter and the car were after us. After all, they've been following us for a long time now. That other thing, with the bright lights. It knocked the helicopter out of the sky. It kept anyone from finding out about the accident. I think it was protecting us and after them." David reasoned.

"Yeah, I think you're right. What do you think the men in the car wanted, besides us dead," Joe clarified.

"I don't know. Maybe they were after the box we have for Sam. Or, they might have wanted some papers I have from one of the men they killed in Gallup."

"What do you think is in the box?" Joe asked.

Joe looked at him intently. "I dunno," David answered. "It is important, though. We can't open it. It's something sacred. We'll know when we're supposed to know."

They resumed their journey in silence, each staring into the night and trying to make sense of their shared experience.

Chapter 21

David regretted leaving Joe as they parted ways at the airport. After all they had been through together, he hated to see Joe leave. David traveled back to South Dakota, thinking of the events of the past week. He did not know what to make of it all. He was not the same man who had left Los Angeles only a few days before.

Dale met him at the airport and drove him out to Lester's house. "Hey, bro." David heard Dale's greeting, and it cheered him. As they bounced along in Dale's pickup, David told Dale of the adventure he had shared with Joe.

The dogs ran out to greet them as they came through the gate. The three men were soon seated around Lester's table.

"Tell me about the trip," Lester said.

"Dale's heard it already," David apologized. "I couldn't keep it to myself."

"I wouldn't have been able to either," Dale assured him. "I'll have to hear it again to believe it anyway."

David recalled for Lester and Dale how he found out the man in Gallup had also been killed. He told them about his meeting with the widow, Elsa, and the mechanic who had seen the car.

He set the box he had brought with him in the center of the table before he continued his narrative.

"This is what I was supposed to bring back for Sam," David told them.

"What's in it," Dale asked.

"I have no idea," David answered. "I only know everything you are about to hear has something to do with this box. I am beginning to think it has something to do with your problems up here, too."

David told them of the strange incident in the cave, and his meeting with Seegook.

"I don't think he is a human at all," David concluded. "Or else I dreamed the whole thing."

"Yeah, well, dreams don't make boxes appear," Lester reminded him.

"Joe and I lost time, too, somewhere between leaving Charlie's and getting back there," David said. He told them about the watches, about Joe's lack of having seen or heard anything in the cave.

"We don't know where we were. It was the oddest feeling," David said.

He paused in thought, adding, "It's even weirder to think about the rest of the day." He told Dale and Lester about the dark car, the helicopter, the speeding aerial light display followed by the explosions. When he told them about the huge fiery diamond-shaped craft that wiped the accident scene clean, Lester and Dale sat in thoughtful silence.

David awoke to the sound of Lester's dogs barking, and the sizzle of sausages on the stove. Dale was already up, sitting at the table with a cup of coffee.

"I have news," Lester announced as he served David coffee and eggs. "We're going into the facility up here tomorrow night."

"How?" David asked in surprise.

"A couple of our plants can get us in," Lester answered. "We'll have to be careful. We'll take in the metal box we found at the crash site and see what it can tell us."

"Maybe it will explain some things about their research up there," Dale said.

"There must be a lot which isn't understood about the ionosphere," David added.

"I heard someone say some of the research into the Northern Lights could be involved in this, too," Dale said.

"Why would the Northern Lights be included?" David asked.

"Scientists and governments have been working on the Aurora up north for quite a few years now," Dale answered. "They shoot rockets up into them and can even make the Aurora visible by whatever it is they send up in the rockets."

"I guess those tests have something to do with the ionosphere, too," David agreed.

"From what I hear, the researchers might be trying to find out how the Aurora disrupts communications and creates energy fields, and devise a way to channel those properties for their own use in weapons," Lester added.

David understood the breadth of the problem they faced. It was possible there were a large number of facilities like this one working on different areas of research. Each could be unaware of the existence or mission of the others, but reporting results to a common person or agency who could have access to the information from them all.

The day was consumed with preparations for the clandestine mission. By the time the lights were out that night, David could not sleep. His anxiety about the coming evening was matched by his confusion about the recent adventures he had survived.

His eyes absently followed the moving patterns of shadows on the floor. His ears registered the breeze and the scraping sound of a branch on the wall outside his window. Then another sound caught his attention. The hoot of an owl reminded him of the night he joined Sam in the sweat lodge. Dale and Sam had called it an announcement of death. It was unsettling to hear it again. David and his two friends were about to embark on a secret and possibly dangerous mission.

Chapter 22

"Can't sleep all day. We've got work to do." Lester's voice broke into David's dream, and his hand shook David's shoulder.

David opened his eyes to see Lester above him, offering him a cup of coffee.

"What time is it?" David asked, rubbing his eyes. "It's still dark." He took the coffee.

"4:30! I barely got to sleep!" David protested. He did not mind, though. The day had promise of excitement and adventure.

David felt a child-like enthusiasm. It made him think of the early mornings when his dad would rustle him from his sleep for an early morning fishing trip. There were those early mornings, too, when he was at camp. They had to rise early to get everything they wanted to do finished in one day. There was something about getting up before the sun. It added urgency, mystery, and excitement to the morning.

The sun was just breaking over the horizon as the three men pulled out of Lester's drive. The dogs howled in unison, ran beside the pickup, then jumped into the back. They propped their front feet on the edge of the pickup and sniffed the wind.

Sam met them at the door of his hut and welcomed them in for coffee. They sat at Sam's table, Lester and Dale talking quietly with Sam. David handed the box he had been given in the cave to Sam. Sam took it and said, "Come."

The men left the hut and walked a short distance toward a cluster of trees where a teepee was standing. Sam entered through the opening and a few moments later, reappeared with the invite for Lester, Dale, and David to come inside.

A fire circle was in the center. The smoke from the fire escaped through the opening at the top of the structure. Sam sat down, and invited the three men to do the same.

When he opened the box, David was shocked to see it contained but one item. Sam lifted it out of the container and handed it to David. It was the very same ivory billiken figure he had presented to Sam a few days before. How had it gone to Arizona, and why had he been asked to return it to Sam? This made no sense.

He handed the shiny smooth ivory back to Sam, the unspoken question in his eyes. Sam set it down on a nearby cot, and David and the others watched in wonder as it began to glow. It seemed to David that it was beginning to transform into something living, but at the same time, a source of radiant light. The shimmering brilliance began to grow until David saw before him something that resembled a life-size billiken shape. As the light began to dim, the form was again transformed, this time into the shape and features of a human being. It looked like old shaman, Koongoosuk, when David last saw him as a child.

Koongoosuk put his "hand" on Sam's shoulder who began to speak. "Seagoyuk," he said to David. Oddly, the voice sounded like Koongoosuk, not Sam.

"Where have you come from?" David asked.

Koongoosuk, speaking through Sam said, "Not from a different planet or star system. We come from a different dimension — a kind of parallel universe. We are spiritual beings, not subject to the physical laws of your universe."

"What do you want of me?" David knew he had been chosen for something, but he didn't know what, or how it was to be accomplished.

"You are not yet ready to know. You are only beginning your training. You succeeded, though, in fulfilling your first test." Koongoosuk's voice came from Sam's moving lips.

"What was my test?" David asked.

"To fulfill this quest," the voice said. "When you were very young, you were already chosen."

"But why me?" David asked.

"Because of your inner spirit, your innocence, and your courage," the voice said. "Few humans have the inner spirit you possess."

"But I don't understand what I am to do. I don't know what is happening," David implored.

"You will know when it is time. Your world is a battleground between many good and evil forces. We have long been involved in trying to rescue humanity from itself and from those who would destroy it by their evil," the voice explained. "In ancient times, humans saw us as angels and demons. Others have seen us as flying dragons and spacemen. You have known, even from your holy books of the wars in heaven. We will win, but not every battle, and not yet. You will help us, and we will help you."

"What am I to do?" David asked again.

"You are to suffer, to learn," the voice said. It seemed almost a promise.

David wondered in awe at the words of the spirit, who began to transform again into light, which was swallowed up by the figure which became a little ivory billiken once more. Lester and Dale were clearly puzzled. They had seen a bright light, but nothing more, and heard sounds but no words. It seemed the message was for David alone of the three men. Sam, though, had been the messenger, as he was now the chief planner of events for the coming evening.

"Go. All is prepared. You must act now." David realized Sam was the orchestrator, the central controller of all the decisions affecting the region and the people in it.

The day progressed and the plans for the night were completed. David knew his own growing nervousness was matched by the intensity of the other men's moods. Sam, now serious and somber, led David, Lester, Dale and the stranger to an ancient sacred place.

Sam began to chant, initiating the ceremonial to ensure their preparation and protection for the uncertainties of the night. Smoke from sage and cedar, like incense, enveloped them in a purifying haze. Like ancient warriors, the men prepared themselves for the unknown.

David's senses were overpowered and he floated in the dreamscape of sight, sound, scent, and sense. The rhythm of the drum and the chanting seemed to echo from some distant past. The fragrance of the smoke, and the feel of the colors on his skin gave David a feeling of fearlessness and courage.

The men filed back, a silent column of warriors, to Sam's hut.

Chapter 23

David, Lester, and Dale left Sam's hut and walked into the night. David smelled the horses and heard their hooves pawing at the earth before their outlines became visible against the sky.

"Have you ever ridden a horse?" Dale asked David.

"It's been a long time," David answered. "My dad used to take my sister and me. He thought it would be good for our education."

"A wise man, your father," Lester said. "He might have saved your life tonight."

Lester smiled, but David knew his comment was serious. David hoped he could remember enough, and feel confident enough to keep his inexperience from putting them all in danger.

"Take this one," Dale said as he brought a tethered pony to David. "She's good with strangers."

"Will she know I can't remember how to ride?" David asked.

"She'll keep up with the others. You won't have to worry about her," Dale answered.

"Let's go." Lester barked the command as he mounted his own pony.

David scrambled onto the back of his pony, and she trotted off with the other two. The line of horsemen moved with silence, stealth, and speed. David, riding between Lester and Dale, regained his confidence. He could not see where they were going, but he trusted the sure-footed gait of his pony on the trail.

They arrived at the rim of a high rock wall which overlooked a broad plain below. In the distance, at the base of the far hill across the valley, David could see the lights of the weapons-testing facility.

Lester led them to a grove of trees in the valley, and they dismounted.

"We'll have to leave the ponies here," he said.

A sliver of moon cast faint light over the plain. It was scant help for them to find their way. On the other hand, the darkness would hide them from view as they approached the base.

The complex was a fortress. It looked to David more like a prison than a research institution. Searchlights cast beams along the walls and the fences surrounding them. Towers overlooked corners and gates. It reminded David of a medieval castle, hiding its secrets within secrets.

This place was not marked on any map. Its expenses would not be found in the government budget reports. It was a world of its own, built on land the existence of which was denied; operated with money which supposedly did not exist; and controlled by people who had no official government sanction.

The three men crouched low as they moved across the night-drenched prairie. The fortress grew larger against the starry night. The first major objective for the three men was to avoid the beacons of light punctuating the darkness.

Lester led them to a ditch near a road leading to the gates of the facility. He directed them with hand signals to hide in the willows lining the bank. They waited.

The lights of a vehicle appeared in the distance. When it was near the men, it slowed, but did not stop. Lester signaled for his companions and the three men rushed from the bank to the back of the truck.

A man was standing in the back of the truck to help the three collaborators scramble into it. Another directed them into hidden cavities where they could remain undetected until they were inside the gates.

David felt claustrophobic locked in his cocoon. The truck swayed as it continued down the road. He felt it stop at the gate, and could hear the exchange of words, the rustling of the papers, and the boots of the guards searching the inside of the truck. He hoped they would not hear his heartbeat, it seemed so loud to him.

He knew they had made it through this obstacle when the truck started moving again. The lid of his coffin-like space was removed, and he emerged to see Dale and Lester breaking out of their cocoons as well. The two plants, the driver of the truck and the man in the back, handed them clothing to make them inconspicuous, and gave them forged identity cards and passes. The truck slowed again, the doors opened, and the three men poured out. A security man wearing a gun at his waist, stepped out of the shadows behind them.

"Moon, how does it look?" Dale whispered.

"Ok so far," Moon whispered back.

The four men walked with an official confidence which hid David's fear. They passed through the checkpoint into the building, much to David's relief The passes had worked.

Moon led them through a series of passageways. David thought they must have looked like mice running through a maze, watching for the cat.

They entered a room filled with flashing lights and huge screens, with maps and figures changing constantly. David looked up, surprised to see the ceiling made into a giant star-map. It reminded him of a planetarium. David had never seen anything like this room. He thought it must have been some kind of command center.

They were not alone. People were working at their computers, and the place was humming with activity. The four men walked into an enclosed cubicle.

A woman sat at the desk, her computer before her. She turned and smiled. Her voice was quiet, her manner efficient.

"You are right on time," she said to Lester.

"We must hurry," Lester said. "David, meet Moon Walks-on-Grass and Autumn Shaw. This is David Seabird. He's joined us."

There was little time for polite introductions. Lester removed the box David had seen at his house. Autumn took it and went to work. Moon watched though the window in Autumn's cubicle for any unwanted visitors.

The rest of the men huddled around Autumn's computer, waiting for her to decipher the mysteries contained in the box salvaged from the destroyed weapon.

"I think we have something here," Autumn said as she bent over her screen.

David could not make out what was on the screen, but Lester and Autumn were excited about the results.

"It looks like we have some important data here," Lester said. "Autumn can connect this to the information she's already put together for us, and we'll have a good picture of the tests and their results."

"Autumn will transfer this data out of here," Dale said to David as she continued to work. "We'll have the information, but the people here won't."

"We'd better get you out soon," Moon told Lester after checking the time.

They left Autumn, still transmitting data from the disk they had brought to her. Moon walked them back through the maze of corridors. They left the building, still safe.

Moon opened the back of the truck intended to smuggle them back out of the gate. Suddenly, a siren split the silence and searchlights sent beams across the plains. The men heard yells from the guards on the walls and at the gates, and they knew they had been discovered.

Lester and Dale had just scrambled into the truck when they heard shots. David felt the impact of the bullet as it lodged in his back. He lurched ahead in pain, his vision already blurred and consciousness slipping away.

Dale jumped out into another hail of gunfire to pull the staggering David to safety. Moon slammed the door shut, yelling to the driver, "Go! I'll hold them off as long as I can!"

The truck rocketed forward. The sudden movement threw David into the side of the truck, and pain shot through his back. Lester and Dale were thrown off balance as the truck rammed through the checkpoint and down the road.

"Are you still with us, buddy?" Lester yelled to David.

"Hanging in there," David managed to mumble back. Dale worked his way over to help make David as comfortable as possible in the circumstances.

Dale ripped off his own shirt and tore strips to make a temporary bandage for David's wound. He could see how the serious the situation that faced them was. Dale looked up at Lester and shook his head in silence.

To David, he offered encouragement, "You're gonna be fine. We'll be there soon."

Sirens continued to blare at the facility, and a security car pursued the escaping truck.

"I think they got Moon," the driver yelled to Lester. "I saw him fall. How are you back there?"

"David's been hit. We'll take him home. Hope Sam can help him," Lester yelled back.

When the truck reached the rendezvous point, it slowed enough for Dale and Lester to jump out. David, groaning in pain, was still conscious and could move. Lester and Dale grabbed David, and they all rolled into the bushes beside the road as the truck sped away.

The security car raced past them. Helicopters hovered overhead. Beams of light flashed before and beyond them, but they had not been seen.

Those in the truck were less fortunate. The car could not overtake them, but the helicopter did. The men hiding by the roadside saw a streak of light shoot from the helicopter. They heard the explosion as it hit the truck, and could see the fireball.

"We've got to get David to help," Dale said.

Lester and Dale supported David's weight between them as they hurried as fast as possible under the circumstances across the valley toward the horses. The sound of helicopters, and the flash of their search beams, surrounded them.

They reached the horses. Lester put David's barely conscious form in front of him on his own horse. Dale led David's horse behind him. The sounds of the helicopters diminished as the men hurried home.

Lester and David reached Sam's hut first. Dale jumped off his pony and ran to the door.

"David's been shot!" Dale yelled as he pounded on the door.

Sam emerged and immediately took control.

"Bring David to the sweatlodge," Sam commanded.

Dale and Lester carried David, by now unconscious, into the sweatlodge and placed him on a mat.

"I don't think he's going to make it, Lester," Dale admitted.

Dale sat next to David's bleeding form and looked down in despair. Lester joined them.

An owl hooted in the distance, calling for David.

Chapter 24

When Sam came into the sweatlodge, he had the box David brought with him from Arizona. Sam took out the billiken ivory carving and started chanting. Soon a bright light began to transform into the human-like form of Old Man Koongoosuk. Dale and Lester watched in wonder as an amazing healing ceremony, the like of which they had never seen before, began.

Both men began to feel lightheaded; they were tired. The heat within the lodge and the rhythm of Sam's chanting made them drowsy. In the hot semi-darkness, Dale and Lester forgot where they were and why they had all gathered there. They began to dream a common dream.

In it, they floated above the scene and watched it from a perch at the top of the sweat lodge. They could see sparks of light dancing around the ceiling like fireflies darting on a summer's night.

The stranger entered and walked to where David was lying lifeless on the mat. Dale, from his imaginary perch, watched. Dale remembered later that he was not surprised when he saw the stranger transform from a man into a unfamiliar creature. Light radiated from the man's head, which turned into glowing circles. His neck stretched into a long rope; his arms extended; his legs transformed into two thin twigs. He seemed to fill the lodge. His features disappeared in a blinding halo. Had David been conscious, he would have recognized "Seagod" whose powers enveloped him and carried away his spirit.

Streams of light seemed to emanate from the creature's head, as he bent and stretched over David's prone body. With one of the long appendages serving as fingers, it reached toward the wound in Dale's back. Electric currents, or what looked to Dale like miniature northern lights moved between the creature's finger and David's body. Dale and Lester dreamed they heard a sizzling sound as the edges of the wound began to dry, to close, and to disappear altogether.

David, though, was unaware of these proceedings. He entered a different world altogether. He heard music, beautiful ethereal music. A great white swan seemed to appear beneath his body, and he was flying on the bird's back. Up through the sweatlodge, as if there had been no roof, over the trees, canyons, and clouds. He lost all sense of fear. He soared through the heavens. He looked down to see the earth receding beneath him and the moon becoming larger and larger. He raced past it, each mountain and crater defined in exact detail. It did not occur to him to wonder how he could fly, or how he could recognize features on the moon he had learned about from schoolboy lessons. The great swan flew into the sun, but here, David began to feel pain. He knew he was dying. He could feel his body being turned inside out. Each bone was separated from the other. David felt it all in excruciating pain.

Then it was over. His body was but a pile of bones. But as he watched, the bones were being put back together. He was being built up again. He stared into the sun, and saw a light even brighter beyond it. The swan began to soar back to the earth, but David could not see it because of the light in his eyes. He shut his eyes to block out the blinding light, but it burned through his eyelids. When he opened them, he saw "Seagod" over him, the brilliant light behind him beginning to fade. He was back in the sweatlodge. The swan was nowhere to be seen, but he could see Dale, Lester, and Sam in the shadows. He also saw Old Man Koongoosuk.

David watched through his haze, as "Seagod" transformed into Seegook. Sam continued to chant as he moved around Dale's body. David was aware of the scent of sage and cedar smoke, and of flashing lights buzzing around his head. He remembered no more.

When David awoke, he was on a mat in Sam's hut. He sat up in surprise, thinking he must have passed out, and tried to remember what he had been drinking. He remembered instead, the events of the night.

He had died, and he had flown to the moon. He had passed the moon and flown into the sun. How could any of this be?

Dale, too, awoke to memories. David had been shot. He remembered the sound; he remembered the journey home. He jumped up from the mat, expecting the worst.

Instead, he saw David, sitting in front of the door, staring blankly into space.

Both men were confused. Had they dreamed the night or was it real? Had David not died before Dale's eyes? Yet, here he sat.

"I thought you were dead," Dale said quietly.

"I was," David answered.

Both men sat together silently for a very long time. Words seemed impossible.

"What happened?" Dale asked.

"I'm not sure, but I know I was dead. I saw things no one living could see. My body was destroyed, I could see that. Yet I was conscious of what I witnessed."

"How was your body destroyed?" Dale asked in wonder at this one who had somehow returned from the world beyond.

"Everything was taken apart — the bones, the flesh. I could feel it all. They were all mixed together, and then put back as if I were recreated."

"That was like a shaman initiation, from what I've heard," Dale said. "Anyway, I don't know how any of this happened, but you don't have a hole in your back this morning."

"Yeah, but I don't know what it means. What I am supposed to do after this?" David asked. "I don't know what is wanted of me, or why this happened to me."

Lester joined them, also confused by the strangeness of the recent events.

"The two strangers — they healed you, David." Lester said.

"I've seen them before," David answered. "In fact, I've been seeing them a lot recently. Old Man Koongoosuk was an old shaman I knew when I was a boy. I guess he's not human after all."

They men sat deep in thought, mulling over the immense ramifications of this revelation.

"And Seegook. I met him only a few days ago, I guess it was. Seems like a lifetime. He showed me a painting he called 'Seagod,' and it was the light you saw last night. I saw it in Arizona. It gave me the box to bring back here. I guess Seegook is not human either."

"I guess we weren't dreaming, anyway," Lester concluded.

Sam brought David to the teepee. They bowed their heads and entered through the low flap. David could see Koongoosuk and Seegook seated on the ground opposite the entry. The space was dimly lit by a ray of light coming through the top of the teepee. The light made a perfect circle on the floor. Sam and David sat on the ground near them.

"You have questions for us, I'm sure." Seegook said to David.

"Who are you both. I thought I knew you, but I don't. Where are you from?" David asked.

"We are visitors to this world. You know it, and have known for some time," Seegook answered.

"Why have you come here?" David asked.

"We are plants from another dimension," Old Man Koongoosuk answered. "Our concern is over damage humans have done to Earth, and to themselves."

"Are you here to help us, then?" David asked.

"We are, but there are others here who are not," Seegook said.

David asked, "Who are they, and what do they want?"

"Do you remember what I taught you before?" Seegook added. "There are good and evil beings, spiritual forces as well as human beings. Some of these are greedy and destructive and seek only their own profit. They care nothing for others."

David found the extent of evil which extended beyond our world depressing.

Koongoosuk added, "There are some evil beings, advising human leaders on earth, who seek the control of your planet and destruction of humanity itself. Some of your leaders are wise, some foolish. It is not difficult for these evil plants to infiltrate your world and bring about chaos and turmoil. Manipulating the earth's atmosphere, including the ozone layer, is only one aspect of their control."

"How are they able to do it?" David asked.

"By utilizing the worst aspects of human nature," Seegook answered. "Humans are too easily led by their negative instincts. They hate more than they love. Greed is more prevalent than compassion. Power over others is sought instead of cooperation."

David answered, "I always thought human nature was basically good."

"That is why infiltration is so easy for them," Seegook said. "Humans are idealistic. They want to believe the best of themselves. Their history is, however, more dismal. It is filled with hatred and destruction. Evil beings from other worlds encourage this behavior. We want to rescue humanity from itself."

"How can you rescue us?" David asked.

"We can warn you of the dangers," the stranger said. "We can monitor the activities which damage your world and ours. We can protect you from the evil ones among you."

Koongoosuk continued after a few moments of silence. "One of our immediate concerns is the testing you and the others here have discovered. The manipulation of the ionosphere may have adverse effects beyond your world. The Earth is not alone. What happens here affects other regions of space."

David sat in silence again. There was little he could say, or even ask. Koongoosuk's words made sense to him.

"You may think Earth is insignificant," Koongoosuk continued, "but what happens here affects everything else. We cannot allow Earth to be destroyed, for it may lead to disastrous consequences for us all."

"Why do you come in the shape of someone I know, a human?" David asked.

"You see us in the shape of someone you trusted, someone who is wise, and who can teach you. I am Old Man Koongoosuk, I don't simply look like him, Seagoyuk," he answered.

"But you are not human are you?" David asked.

"No, like Seegook, I am a spiritual being, not bound by physical laws of your universe," Koongoosuk answered.

"Have you been coming here for long?" David asked.

"Eons," Seegook said. "There have always been those few among you who have recognized us. We are the messengers. We ride on the winds. Our words bring both warning and comfort."

"Why have you chosen to come here?" David asked.

"We work with people like Sam and Charlie. Their ancestors also knew who we were. They respect the earth and the sky. They accept the things not seen in the visible world."

"How did I come to be involved in all this?" David asked.

"You were chosen for a task."

"Chosen for what task?" David did not understand Seegook was saying to him.

"The first task was to show obedience, to bring the gift from Charlie to Sam," Seegook said.

"Yes, why was all of that trip necessary?" David asked.

"It was part of your quest," Koongoosuk said. "The gift was not necessary for me, but for you. Your mission gave you experience, understanding, and preparation you would not otherwise have had."

"What am I being prepared to do?" David asked.

"You will be a messenger," Seegook replied. "You will help to tell others of the dangers facing earth. You must confront evil in the world and work to prevent Earth's catastrophic destruction."

"I don't know how," David said.

"You will when the time comes," Seegook assured him. "Our helpers have always been here. Throughout your human history, there have been crises which could have destroyed the earth. The catastrophe has, so far, been averted. You must help us now."

"I will try," David said. "But why don't you announce yourselves to the world?"

"Most humans could not cope with this revelation," Koongoosuk answered. "Many would flock to our evil counterparts. They would seek ever more power through supernatural means, as some are now. If all humans had the same compassion and reverence for life as Charlie and Sam have, we could reveal ourselves. We could assist your earthly governments in the betterment of life. It is not possible yet."

"Do human governments know about your existence?" David asked.

"Of course," Seegook answered. "Some know and have chosen to seek the power of evil. They do not understand the danger they face. They believe they will become the rulers, but their masters will destroy them."

"Who are these masters?" David asked.

"Those I mentioned before. Those who seek destruction. They consider humans as nothing more than their slaves, and stores of genetic material. Those whose weapons crashed, the ones who are seeking to disrupt the ionosphere, are working with those evil masters. It will result in their own destruction. We are here, hidden as plants in a strange world, far from our own."

"Why do you call yourself a plant?" David asked.

"Biological plants on earth feed the people of earth," Koongoosuk said. "They provide its oxygen. They bring life and comfort. We are not here to find out your secrets. We are here to protect life."

"I will help. I promise." David said.

"You are not alone. Think of us as your guardian angels."

Chapter 25

David's thoughts were consumed with the conversation he had with Koongoosuk and Seegook. He did not feel like talking. The events of the past few days were like a dream, but he knew they were real. He could not imagine what it would mean to his life, though.

This was no longer a mere assignment to report a story. Would he be taken seriously by anyone if he told them what he had learned? How would Ward react when David came to him with an account of all that had happened? Would he think the assignment had simply been too much for David, and that now the results of pressure were showing through? What kind of story could David write, and still be believed?

There was Holly to consider. She was sensible, earthbound. She often showed her disdain for the sensational and unlikely stories associated with aliens and UFOs. He could see her laughing at the checkout stand, pointing to the headline, "Speaker of the House Meets With Aliens!" Would she be embarrassed if she saw his byline on such an implausible story? On the other hand, if what he had been told was true, he would have to speak the truth if he had love for Holly, his family, his employer, or any fellow human being.

He had been given a purpose, a task. He was becoming involved in the destiny of the planet. How could he return to the mundane, everyday life he had lived, no matter how much he had enjoyed it. Life for him had changed. He had become another being.

From what he understood, the very ability of Earth to sustain human life might be threatened. One thing could lead to another. He remembered the reports about the hole in the ozone layer. It not only affected the atmosphere, but the food chain. If one creature failed, then the rest were threatened. If they found food enough to survive, they could be killed by cancers as a result of the destruction of the filters within the atmosphere.

Seegook's words were true. One person's choices could never be confined to his or her life alone. They affect everything around them. Those, too, must affect all they touch. Like the rock in the pool, the influence of one small event spreads ever wider until the whole has been changed.

David thought about Sam and Charlie. He could understand now why these non-humans came to them. The whole reason for Sam's and Charlie's respect for nature and their striving for balance was to preserve order. They taught their people to take no more than necessary for survival because they understood the importance of each animal and plant to the maintenance of nature's balance.

Sam and Charlie taught their people to seek harmony with nature rather than domination of it because they understood that domination always leads to destruction; and destruction of one part eventually destroys the whole. They had learned self-preservation must come by rejecting greed and power over others. Only by seeking harmony and cooperation with the whole, instead of enriching the self, could one survive.

"You are quiet," Dale said, drawing David out of his silence.

"I was just thinking about how much damage can be done by people trying to improve on nature."

"Anything in particular?" Dale asked.

"I guess I was thinking about a lot of things," David said. "I don't know where to start."

They drove on while David began to talk about how easy balance can be destroyed, beginning with trivial matters.

"Take advertising, for instance. Someone comes up with a new product, say whale bone corsets. The advertising tells the women they will be more attractive to men when they squeeze out their insides with these bone cages. What happens? The women die or get sick from abusing their bodies with these things, and the whales almost become extinct so manufacturers can sell them and make a profit while the fad rages. In the end, who benefits?"

"The manufacturer," Dale said. "He makes a profit."

"Yes, but only for a short time," David said. "He can't make a profit on something after it becomes extinct. He'd be better off himself if he made less in the short run, and had not been so greedy that he destroys his own source of income. Nobody wins that way. Not the manufacturer, not the hunter, not the women, and not the whale. It starts as something trivial, but one thing leads to another until it becomes an issue of greater magnitude of destruction."

"Yeah, it almost happened with the buffalo, too," Dale said.

"Sure. Instead of taking only what was needed for survival, people started slaughtering them for profit. They became a commodity instead of a living part of nature. People started killing so many, the buffalo couldn't keep up any more."

"Most people only cared when it was almost too late to do anything," Dale added.

"Somebody was making a profit from killing buffalo, feeding railway workers," David continued. "The railway goes in, so it can bring in more people to farm or mine. More people have to cut more trees to make houses, farms, mines, and towns. After the trees are stripped from the hills, a big rain washes the topsoil into the stream and kills all the fish. Again, one thing just leads to another."

Dale and David bounced along in silence thinking about the ease with which life can be destroyed.

"Think of it Dale," David said. "Some king last century found a pretty feather, and stuck it in his hat. After that, everyone else wanted one. You know the fashion only ended when all the birds were dead. We killed a whole species of birds just to put feathers in hats."

"It's like our dams out west," Dale said. "No one out here used to need electricity, but now everyone has it. It has to come from somewhere, so they dam up a river. The river floods people's homes and sacred lands. You end up with all this water, so you can start growing crops in the desert, which means more farmers can move in. After more people move in, you need more water to keep them all going, so you start having fights over water rights, the fish die, then everything with the people collapses, too. You are right, it all ties together."

David said, "The politicians, even the people who are most affected never think the rest of the equation is important until somebody finds out the whole base of the economy is about to collapse. Only then do they start to think they might become extinct, too. You remember the quarrels between Spain and Canada, or Canada and the U.S. over who has the right to take the last fish in the ocean?"

"Yes," Dale answered, "and I was reading how the destruction of the rain forest is changing flood and drought patterns."

"I saw it, too, and how the burning the of trees there might be disrupting the earth's atmosphere," David added.

David had never thought before of so many examples of good ideas gone wrong. Usually, they went wrong because someone was making money at the expense of someone or something else. There was the pattern again; domination, greed, and power over others could only lead to self-destruction in the end.

"Look at the problems with nuclear accidents and disposal of nuclear waste," David said.

"The same could be said of all those chemicals and biological experiments meant to be directed against other humans in warfare," Dale added.

"Certainly," David said. "Remember Three Mile Island and Chernobyl? You know, they had to keep Eskimos and Saamis from eating their caribou and reindeer meat after Chernobyl."

"I remember reading about it," Dale said. "The fallout from the accident in the Ukraine poisoned the lichens and other plants the reindeer ate in Scandinavia. The radiation poisoned the meat of their bodies, so they weren't safe to eat."

David added, "I hear there are nuclear submarines just rusting away because no one can afford to maintain them. They could be worse than Chernobyl. I was reading the other day about all the problems the U.S. has trying to dispose of all the nuclear warheads they are supposed to get rid of under the test ban treaties."

"What did it say?" Dale asked.

David answered, "Something about how easy it was to destroy the shell, so everyone thinks we've got fewer and fewer warheads, right on schedule. The truth, though, is no one knows what to do with the bomb part of the thing. They are storing all these thousands of bombs with all the dangerous nuclear material until they can find some way to dispose of them safely."

Dale added, "It isn't safe, even without all the nuclear waste. Remember the Exxon Valdez and Desert Storm?"

"Yes," David said. "I remember oil companies for years told everyone not to worry about oil spills, because by the time they might be apt to have an accident, which they were sure would be never, they'd have the technology figured out to clean it up. They didn't start working on how to do it until the oil spill happened. Before then, it wasn't economical to do it."

The men were silent with their thoughts for a few moments.

Dale said, "I've been thinking for a long time about the way things are falling apart so fast. It's why I'm fighting against the tests at the factory over here. They aren't just working on science and industry. They have the future of our world at stake."

David said, "It's so easy for things to go wrong. I was horrified to hear about the biological testing at a facility near Washington, D.C. They imported some monkeys from Africa to use for their tests, but they were all infected with a killer virus. I guess they were worried themselves when they realized how horrible the epidemic might have been if it had been a strain humans could contract through the air."

"Sam is right when he teaches us to respect nature," Dale said.

"Yes, it appears there are practical as well as moral reasons to do so," David added. "I suppose we should not believe we are the only ones to face these problems, though. The stranger told me humans have always had to make these choices. He said the earth has nearly been destroyed many times."

"I think it is true," Dale said.

"I guess he was trying to tell me I may not be able to make right everything that is wrong with the world, but I have an individual responsibility to speak out against it," David said. "I owe it to the rest of the world to take responsibility for my own actions, and to consider others instead of only myself."

"We all must if we are going to survive," Dale added.

David concluded, "I must do what is right, no matter what it might cost me personally."

Chapter 26

They drove into Lester's yard to be met by the barking dogs. The animals jumped at the car and ran circles around the two men as they walked to the door. Lester welcomed them in and offered them coffee.

Lester said, "We've been trying to find out as much as we can. We still have a lot of work to do, though. Autumn is at the computer now."

"Is it safe for Autumn to be here?" David asked. He remembered the violence of the previous night, of the word that Moon had been killed. He wondered if the authorities from the facility might connect Autumn to the intruders.

"We have to take the risk," Lester replied as he poured coffee for Dale and David. "I think they already know about us, but we're probably still safe here on the reservation for a while."

"Why would being on the reservation help?" David asked.

"Remember, as far as the military goes, they are a secret facility. They aren't looking for any kind of publicity about what they are up to," Lester said.

"I guess they probably wouldn't want to expose themselves by coming after you if there was any other way to silence you," David agreed.

"The reservation has some special advantages," Dale said. "We have our own authorities, our own courts and police. The government must abide by some of its own rules here, even if they have broken treaties. It's harder for them to take arbitrary action on the reservation today. They have to deal with public opinion, human rights organizations, and their own laws."

"Will Autumn be able to get back in safely?" David asked.

"I think so," Lester answered. "We'll have to be careful, and so will she. You may be in the most danger of all."

"Why?" David asked.

"Someone has been following you all along, right from the start," Dale said.

"They knew you were coming out here almost before you did," Lester added. "They know you have access to the press. You could broadcast their secrets, and they would be secret no more."

"I haven't so far," David said.

"Maybe not, but how will they know you won't at sometime?" Dale said.

"Besides, you still have to get home. You have to leave the reservation to get there," Lester said.

"We can't worry about this right now," David concluded. "What have you learned?"

Lester said, "Autumn was able to transmit the data to her colleague. He's still working on it, but it looks like we'll have results from their tests when he's finished. I think they've pieced together some of the telecommunications angles, too."

"Any names?" David asked.

Lester answered, "We know a big conglomerate is involved somehow. It looks like a shadow government working with big business interests to bypass the law."

"I might have guessed as much," David sighed, depressed at the recurring sequences of private and public attempts to gain power and money over the years.

"One of the companies we think we've identified as a controller is based in Seattle, GALCOM," Lester said. "The military side of the operation, we think, is controlled by a certain Nicholas Losskey. He seems to be a colonel on a mission to save the government from itself. He is in charge of the shadow government. GALCOM is just one of the enterprises financing his secret activities."

"What is GALCOM's role?" David asked.

"They are involved in contracts," Lester answered. "We think this involved fraud and money-laundering as well. GALCOM has its own interests, too."

"What do you mean?" Dale asked.

Lester answered, "It looks like GALCOM is financing Losskey's secret operations with the profits it makes from legitimate and fraudulent contracts. We think, though, GALCOM, is supplying their own security people to guard Losskey's secret testing sites, like ours out here. It was a surprise."

"Yes, I see what you mean," David said. "We don't know if Losskey is controlling GALCOM, or GALCOM is controlling Losskey."

"What does GALCOM do?" Dale asked.

"From what we know so far, just about everything. Their main business is telecommunications, computing technology, and space science. I think GALCOM came from an earlier and smaller business, Galaxy Communications. We think the weapon belonged to them, and it was launched secretly by Losskey's people."

"You said the main business was telecommunications. What are the other ones?" David asked.

"They have interests in energy. They've financed some research into non-traditional energy sources," Lester said. "They're also interested in chemical and biological weapons technology and genetics."

Autumn had joined them at the table and added, "They certainly are involved in the ionosphere testing. Most of the research has a cover of legitimacy, but I think there is a lot under the surface we'll be discovering for some time to come."

They talked long into the night, trying to determine how each individual could contribute most effectively to their cause. When David was at long last able to sleep, he could not rest.

He heard gunfire crashing through his head; he was running but going nowhere, while his tormentors pressed in ever closer. He watched aliens battle in the stars, and like a pawn, he was helpless. He could not move; only be moved by another's hand. He woke up to find himself wound tightly in his sheet, but freeing himself gave him no comfort from his nightmare.

He got up and walked outside, hoping to breathe again. One of the dogs stretched from its sleep and walked over to join him on the step. It sat beside him, content to have David stroke its head and back. The dog's company calmed David, too.

He gazed up at the night sky and wondered which of the twinkling stars might not be a star at all. instead, it could be some alien's mother-ship, waiting to retrieve her plants from their hostile and strange surroundings. He heard the sounds of the night. it was so peaceful, so normal. The wind rustled through the leaves and the trees swayed. He heard the babble of a brook nearby.

Two glowing eyes stared at him from the path. The dog bristled and growled, but opted for David's attention and the comfort of the moment to chasing the raccoon. After it scrambled off, the dog settled down, and the night returned to its quiet peace.

Far off in the distance, David saw clouds along the horizon light up with silent lightning. He was fascinated with the thought that he could see the lightning, but he could not hear its thunder. How many light signals already announced earth's inhabitants to the universe? Our presence was as obvious as the the flashes of lightning on clouds against a night sky.

He was still sitting on the step when he heard birds welcome the morning. The sky was ablaze with pinks and reds. The first beams of light broke above the horizon to flood the yard with the new day. Everything seemed fresh, filled with hope. David, too, was hopeful as he witnessed the arrival of the dawn.

It was more difficult than David expected to say good-bye to Lester. If all went well, they would see each other again. They would still be working together for a long time to come, if they made it through this crisis.

Dale saw David to the gate where the two men said good-bye until next time. David almost expected to see someone following him, or to be paged again with some strange message. Instead, he boarded a flight, with normal passengers, making normal trips to their normal destinations. He fell asleep and found the rest the previous night had withheld from him.

Chapter 27

David had time to spare between flights at Salt Lake City. Unhurried and unworried, he wandered from one concourse to the next passing the main ticket counters. He was almost unaware of the two men who approached him until they spoke.

"Mr. Seabird, please come with us," the taller one spoke while the other man watched.

"Who are you?" David asked. "Why should I go with you?" David felt the hair on the back of his neck, a warning of danger.

"We are with National Security," the man replied. "We need you to answer some questions."

David had no intention of going any place with them. He tried his best to look confident, and struggled not to betray his anxiety with his voice.

"I have a plane to catch," he told them. "I don't have time to answer questions."

"Mr. Seabird, you do not seem to realize the seriousness of your position," the second man said. "We are authorized to arrest you if you will not come with us."

"Who gave you that authority, on what charges?" David asked. "I want to see some identification."

The men took out badges and the first said, "We are empowered by the U.S. government to conduct an investigation in matters of interest to national security."

David had no way of knowing if the identifications were real or forged. He could think of no reason they might legally detain him.

"On what grounds do you think you could arrest me?" David asked. He was defiant, almost sarcastic.

The tall man was solemn as he recounted the various crimes. "You could be charged with destruction of government property; illegal trespass; conspiracy to commit a felony; murder; espionage and treason against the United States."

"Who have I killed?" David asked in disbelief.

"Moon Walks-on-Grass and Paul Rosenburg," the man answered.

David sat in stunned silence. He had not expected this, of all things. They could place him at the scene of both men's murders. He had no believable alibi. He had been followed to Mt. Rushmore. He could tell the truth, but they could twist it into a different scenario. They could say he went there to kill Rosenburg. It would be his word against theirs, whoever they were.

How could he defend himself against charges of Moon's murder? They could say espionage was the reason he was there, and that he had killed Moon who was carrying out his security duties. Who would believe they were the ones who killed Moon?

David decided to go with them. He walked down the concourse, one man on each side of him. He assumed they were armed. David already felt like a prisoner. They came to a doorway, and the tall man told David to turn. The three men walked out the door, down a flight of steps, and out onto the tarmac where a small jet waited. David entered the jet, and prepared to journey to his unknown destination. It was the longest flight of his life.

David knew the were flying northwest, and he recognized Seattle as they descended through the broken clouds. They landed, and the jet taxied to where a long black limousine waited on the tarmac. The two men accompanied David to the car.

David could determine nothing more about his circumstances. He remembered Lester's description of GALCOM, and the fact it was based in Seattle made him think someone from the organization as behind his abduction.

The limousine disappeared into a building downtown, and David was escorted to the elevator. It had only one button, the penthouse suite.

David emerged from the elevator into brilliant light. The walls had dissolved around him and he realized he was high above the city. The glass skin of the building revealed the mountains and water in all their beauty.

David was brought into a large, comfortable room and told to wait. He was allowed to sit in one of the fine leather chairs and survey his surrounding. The wall opposite the glass skin soared to a high ceiling and itself contributed to the lightness and airiness of the room. It was broken by a fireplace. The mantle had a number of photographs and framed certificates, lauding the achievements of Glaaxy Communications.

He had been right. All this luxury and opulence belonged to the man in control of Galaxy Communications, and he was about to be presented to him.

The tall man disappeared through a closed door. He returned a few moments later and told David to come with him. David was brought into the immense private suite of Mr. Julian St. Germaine.

St. Germaine was handsome and elegant, but at the same time had a cruel demeanor. His graying temples added a distinguished touch, his expensive tailored suits announced a man of prestige and wealth. Yet, he stared down his long nose with eyes that were cold and shrewd.

"Sit down, Mr. Seabird," he commanded David in a smooth, deep, but cold and unearthly voice.

"No, thank you," David insisted. "I'd rather stand."

"Fine," St. Germaine said. "I think you will sit before we have finished here."

David stared at St. Germaine. St. Germaine was somehow transparent, not figuratively, but literally. David could see through him. St. Germaine had no skeletal structure.

"So," David concluded, "This is one of them. Someone who is not human at all."

He was not terrified by the thought. In fact, it somehow strengthened his resolve to fight against this creature, whatever he was.

Two men besides St. Germaine and David were in the room. One, dressed in an expensive business suit, was introduced as Mr. Adams.

"Our attorney," St. Germaine explained.

The other was in military dress. St. Germaine introduced him as Col. Losskey of the National Security Administration.

St. Germaine continued, "We are concerned about your activities, and those of your friends. We need to talk about your attitude."

David stood still, staring straight ahead. He remembered his own experiences and was not about to look nervous or upset. He had, after all, already experienced death. What could this creature do to him. He stood confidently, maintaining a psychological advantage over the human beings in the room. He could show them he was more than the equal of this arrogant being. David resolved to say as little as possible, and give nothing to St. Germaine.

St. Germaine circled David as he spoke. David found him condescending and cruel. His suave manners and elegant dress could not disguise the man's evil, grasping nature. His smile was cold, calculating, and menacing.

"You and your friends stole property from one of our atmospheric experiments involved in an unfortunate accident. We'd like to have it back," St. Germaine declared.

David stood silent and unmoved.

"You have killed one of our security guards at our research facility," St. Germaine added to the charges.

David clamped his teeth to keep from shouting it was he, not David, who was responsible for Moon's death.

Instead, he controlled his voice and said, "You are holding me here against my will. You have no right to keep me here."

"Aren't you concerned about your friends?" St. Germaine asked with a sneer.

David knew it was a bluff, or at least he wanted to believe it was. He stared at the wall and bit his cheek.

St. Germaine conferred with Col. Losskey for a few moments while David stood waiting, still staring straight ahead.

St. Germaine decided on a different approach. He softened his voice as he said, "Let's be reasonable, Mr. Seabird. We're on the same side. Let's sit down and think about the best interests of the world, here."

David turned his head and looked at St. Germaine. David said, "I'm afraid you think your interests are best for the world."

"Is it so terrible, then?" St. Germaine said. "We need the world. We don't want to destroy it."

He continued, "We are concerned with the future of the planet. Let me explain."

He sat down at the table and motioned to the chair beside him. David refused.

"There are many in this world working against the best interests of the planet," St. Germaine said. "We are trying to make a better world for all. We see the promise of the future. Many are too blind to fulfill the promise. They cannot be progressive."

St. Germaine paused, waiting for a response from David. He got none, so continued his account of his business, "Many ignorant people work against our projects. They don't know what the business means, how it will improve their lives in the long run. They only think of today. Because they are against us, and they twist the facts about our enterprise, we must work in secret. We are not doing anything wrong. We are only trying to continue our important research. We do it for the good of the earth."

David still said nothing, but he wanted to tell St. Germaine he could not believe his experiments could benefit humanity if it destroyed the ability of life to sustain itself.

St. Germaine continued, "There are others, like you. You are ignorant and naive. You threaten our progress by your well-meaning but misdirected interference."

David thought St. Germaine sounded like a ranting dictator, sure of his own good intentions while he destroyed people.

"Since you do not yet understand, I will give you an example," St. Germaine said. "A few years ago, the ability to decide the world's future rested with those who controlled the oil. It is more complex today. Oil is still important. Alternative energy is important. We must plan for new developments in genetic research, medical technology. Most of all, we must have access and control of information. Whoever controls information controls the earth. Whoever controls the earth has the power to make it better."

David thought St. Germaine sounded so convinced of the high morality of his ideals.

David said, "Do you think a benevolent dictatorship is in order for the Earth?"

St. Germaine snorted with disdain.

"Democracy is only a word," he said. "It is perfectly meaningless as a governing system. Democracies are absolutely inefficient and corrupt. One cannot run a country or a business by pandering to the lowest common denominator. One should never try to please the majority at the expense of the rest of the population."

David said nothing.

"Why do you think political campaigns are run the way they are?" St. Germaine asked. "They try to please everyone with the words each individual or special interest wants to hear. They know if they were to keep every contradictory promise they made to get elected, it would destroy the country. They must use the system to achieve a position within which they can make a difference."

"Why have you kidnapped me?" David asked St. Germaine, changing the subject.

"You have not been kidnapped," St. Germaine protested. "We only want what is ours. We want to work with you in your noble goals to better the world, and to show you where you have been deceived."

"Who has deceived me?" David asked.

"You have been brainwashed by a group of terrorists seeking the overthrow of the government." Col. Lasskey spoke for the first time.

"What?" David stammered. This was a new angle on his activities of the past week.

The colonel continued, "You have been in the company of a group of Indian dissidents. They keep claiming land belongs to them which doesn't. The government has been generous to them. It has allowed them many rights and privileges it does not give the rest of its citizens. They can have their own tribal courts and their own police forces. They are exempt from certain taxes, and on and on. Still, they rebel against the government."

David disagreed, but said nothing.

Losskey continued, "This group you have been with has abused its special status. It has harbored fugitives from justices and used the reservation as a base to plan and carry out terrorist attacks on government property, and against government agencies."

St. Germaine said, "We know all about your movements, and those of your friends. We know when you arrived in South Dakota, and when you left. We know you went to Arizona and to New Mexico. We know when you returned. You cannot hide your actions, so there is no point in denying them."

David looked at St. Germaine and said slowly, "Why are you interested in following me?"

"Do you remember what I said a minute ago?" St. Germaine asked. "Information is the key. He who has information has power. You get information through communications technology. It is the future. We can learn anything about anyone when necessary. Let me give you a little demonstration."

St. Germaine walked to a terminal, typed in a few commands and within a few minutes began to tell David about himself.

"I can tell you which day you bought dinner for two in Los Angeles. You paid for it with your American Express card. I can tell you how much you spent, and what your current balance is."

David was not too surprised by the revelation.

St. Germaine continued, "I can tell you what you bought at the grocery store, and how much you paid on any given day."

David was only slightly more surprised by the fact St. Germaine knew this. Of course, the items he purchased were scanned into some account, along with the debit card he used to pay for them. "I know what kind of pets you own, what neighborhood you live in, the average income of your neighborhood, what books and newspapers you read, when you last saw your doctor and what, if anything was wrong with you."

David realized what living in the computer age might mean to someone like St. Germaine. It was a terrifying revelation.

"I can make a profile on you or any one else I want to know about, and within reason, I can predict what you will do in almost any circumstance," St. Germaine concluded. "I can tell you who you call, where you call from, and how long you talk. In some cases, or if I want to know badly enough, I can find out what you say in any of those conversations. I can do it all, and legally, with the wonders of communication."

St. Germaine apparently did not know about David's flight to the sun, or his communications with Seegook and Koongoosuk, however. There must be some things that not even St. Germaine could find out with all the technology in the universe.

St. Germaine reveled in his glory, "Information is the key. It is power. You cannot resist us. Don't you think you would prefer to be on our side?"

"I'm not on anyone's side," David said.

"Everyone is on someone's side," St. Germaine said. "By choosing to do nothing, you make a choice. Let me put it to you this way. You might think you have a good story about what you found in South Dakota. You don't. People don't want to hear it. They are tired of government secrets and cover-ups. They want to think their government is still doing some good. The only power they have is the vote. All they can do is throw out one politician and replace him with another. They don't want any more discouragement and disappointment."

David said nothing, but he knew St. Germaine was right on this point at least.

St. Germaine continued, "You think you came across another story. Are you going to call it 'Alien Space Invaders'?"

"What do you know about 'aliens,' as you call them?" David asked.

He could understand Sam's and Charlie's concern about the state of the earth. It was being run by people like St. Germaine, people who were more concerned with personal wealth and power than any true benefit to earth's inhabitants. He could see how someone like St. Germaine would think little of destroying the earth's atmosphere and ionosphere, or any other resources for a short-term gain. He probably considered people expendable, too. He would do anything to satisfy his own greed.

"We know they exist, but it is not necessary to announce it to the world," St. Germaine. "It would create a panic. It is far better to work with them, come to an agreement on how to utilize the earth's resources for both of our benefits."

David thought St. Germaine's statement was a bit too ironic. the fact David was able to see through his physical structure indicated that St. Germaine was himself a stranger to the earth.

St. Germaine continued, "Like your terrorist friends, some of the aliens are working against us. Your Indian friends are hiding them, too. We know it. We haven't quite found the solution to the problem yet, but we will."

"If you can tell everything about me, how come you can't find out about them?" David asked.

St. Germaine looked angry. "They are out of the information loop. Some don't have phones, or use credit. They stay on the reservation. It's harder to get information, but we will."

"What is it you want from me?" David asked.

"We want what belongs to us," St. Germaine said. "We want you to work for us."

"I get to live in exchange for selling my soul?" David asked.

"There are worse things. You could help us change the world. You could help eliminate the competition and resistance against our programs. You know what they are doing out there on the reservation, and could help us break up the terrorist gangs."

David asked, "What if I decide to write a story about all of this, including your invitation for me to come to Seattle?"

St. Germaine and the other two men laughed out loud. St. Germaine said, "What kind of story do you think you would write? Are you going to tell them all about the UFO's and aliens? Are you going to tell them about secret government operations which don't exist. They wouldn't you know, by the time anyone tried to confirm your story. Besides, this is not about reporting a story anyway."

David knew it was true. It wasn't about a story anymore.

St. Germaine continued, "If you did write a story, we could turn it into something believable. Why do you think we have such interest in the film and television industry. We have spent years convincing the human race that there are other forms of life in the universe. You will have half who believe in your story, but can do nothing about it, and half who could do something but think you are crazy."

"What kind of progress do you think your testing brings?" David asked. "Don't you think you could cause permanent damage to the earth through what you are doing?"

"How do you think humans have discovered cures for diseases, and created new medicines," St. Germaine said. "How have they learned to grow more food on marginal lands, find new energy sources, revolutionize labor? Humanity has the best standard of living ever. It is all the result of testing. Testing has given us safer products, longer and better lives."

St. Germaine was circling David again, caught up in his own speech. "Do you want to go back to gathering wood on the beach for your fire every night? If it hadn't been for people like me, you would be living in the stone age. We are working with our allies from other worlds to create new and better products, devise ways of traveling and sending information through space, to set up colonies elsewhere in the universe. Thousands of years from now, they will remember me and thank me, not your friends. They are too tied to the past to live in the present, much less see the future."

The colonel stood and pushed a button. The door opened. The tall man who brought David to Galaxy Communications came into the room. St. Germaine gave one last bit of advice to David.

"You think about this, Mr. Seabird. You could have a good future ahead of you. You could have none. We need you to join us. We will win in the end. But it is up to you."

The interview was over. David was escorted back to the limousine. He was driven to a downtown park and the car stopped.

"We will be in touch for your decision." The tall man opened the door and let David out. The limousine sped away.

David walked to a bench and sat down. Slightly disoriented and troubled, David felt distressed. What could he do? There was his family to consider, his work, his friends, Holly. On the other hand, what good were any of his human attachments and aspirations in the face of such perilous times. He was no longer a simple reporter, living and loving as a normal human being, unaware of the world and its dangers. He had been chosen for a task, a purpose, and his human loves could not be well-served if he rejected all he had been taught the last few days — or was it centuries?

Derelicts wandered past and settled themselves into their sleeping places for the night. In the corner, a bearded man in tattered clothes carried a sign that seemed strangely appropriate to David just then, "Repent, the end of the world is at hand!"

A man sat down next to David. When David looked up to respond to his request for change, David saw it was no man at all.

Seegook was beside him. Without speaking, David heard Seegook answer his own unspoken question.

"We have always been here, and will be until the war is over. you may not recognize us, but as it is written in one of your ancient texts, 'Many have thereby entertained angels unaware'."